A CHANCE FOR LOVE

BOOK 36 THE AMISH BONNET SISTERS

SAMANTHA PRICE

D1522648

CHAPTER 1

*W*ilma stared in shock as she saw Obadiah step out of Eli's buggy and come her way. She glanced at her plain dress, hardly fit to receive visitors. It had never crossed her mind that Obadiah would come to her doorstep, especially since it had been decades since they'd seen each other.

Obadiah stood below Wilma as she peered over the porch railings. "It has been a while," he said with a broad smile.

He was her first love, but he couldn't have guessed at the magnitude of his effect on her. "You're Obadiah," was all she could manage to say.

He gestured behind him to Eli. "We apologize for stopping by unannounced like this, but Eli was certain you wouldn't mind."

Wilma smiled brightly. His words were spoken so effortlessly, as if he'd rehearsed them beforehand.

"I'm glad you did," she spoke warmly.

Obadiah moved nearer to Wilma, and her heartbeat quickened. He was as tall and attractive as she remembered him, only this time with a few extra strands of silver in his hair.

"You haven't changed at all, Wilma," he said.

Flustered, she murmured a humble thank you as memories of simpler times resurfaced; rolling hills beneath the sun's rays, delicious pastries like whoopie pies, and an uncomplicated life without struggles.

When Obadiah tenderly clasped her hand in his, unexpected vibrations coursed through her veins. His grip was firm yet compassionate simultaneously.

Eli's voice disrupted the tranquil moment. "Wilma," he said, "it is good to see you back. This is my cousin Obadiah."

"Oh yes, I remember him from years ago." She reluctantly withdrew her hand and smiled.

Eli ran his fingers through his beard pensively. "Ah yes, of course. He used to live around here."

Wilma studied Obadiah closely, comparing the present version of him to the one she recalled from long ago. He had grown so tall in the meantime and was clean-shaven—leading Wilma to wonder whether he had ever married or if his wife had passed away. Without any words, she continued to look at him in awe, captivated by him.

Wilma felt uncomfortable when she thought about how shabby she appeared next to him in her tattered clothes. She rarely wore this dress anymore; it was fit for nothing other than the trash.

She couldn't allow them into her home; they would notice the dirty laundry strewn on her living room couch. It would give them the wrong sense that she was sloppy and negligent.

Not a good look!

Ada, Krystal, and Wilma had recently returned from Cherish's farm, and Wilma still had chores to take care of at home. Although Debbie had assisted while they were gone, the house wasn't in the condition Wilma wanted it to be.

Where was Ada this morning?

She usually would have already arrived by now; if she were here, the awkwardness Wilma felt would dissipate with her presence.

Eli chuckled upon seeing Obadiah and Wilma together. "You two look like you just saw ghosts from the past," he joked. Wilma felt her cheeks flush as Eli caught her staring at his cousin.

"Yes," she said quietly. "I didn't expect to see a ghost of the past."

Obadiah explained, "Wilma and I are old friends; we used to be close before my family moved away."

"You never said anything," Eli remarked.

"That's because I didn't know the widow from the apple orchard you mentioned was Wilma," Obadiah told him.

Eli nodded and said, "Well, we're all here now."

Now things were even more tense; Wilma didn't want to be described only as a widow from an orchard —she had her own life and story to tell. What had Eli

3

meant by that and what had he told Obadiah about her?

Or had Eli mentioned her in such a way because he was interested in her as more than just a friend? Ada was always teasing her about that possibility.

Wilma glanced up the road, hoping again for some sign of her friend before she turned her attention back to the men. "What a beautiful day. How about we sit here on the porch, and I'll get some refreshments for us?"

"That will be fine, Wilma. Then you can think up some jobs we can do for you. We're both willing to do anything that needs a man's attention. Aren't we?" Eli asked Obadiah.

"Yes. We're ready for anything." Obadiah nodded.

Wilma chuckled. "Well, don't be concerned about the jobs. You can get ready for hot tea, or would you prefer coffee?"

"Coffee for me, please, Wilma," Obadiah said.

"I'll have the same." Eli gave a nod as he walked toward one of the porch chairs.

Once the men sat, Wilma set the broomstick she'd been clutching in one hand against the deck's railing and entered the house.

While her stomach was flip-flopping, she filled the teakettle with water. It had been a long time since she had experienced this sensation, and she'd been sure she'd never feel it again.

Was it destiny bringing them back together?

Wilma dismissed the idea, reminding herself

Obadiah could already be engaged, and he wouldn't be interested in her anyway. Maybe he was married and hadn't been able to grow a beard for some reason.

She was just a young teenager then, and he wouldn't have returned her love.

But she couldn't help her curiosity about why Obadiah was there.

Wilma shook her head, trying to push away her intrusive thoughts. She was being silly, wasn't she?

She couldn't wait for Ada to arrive. Ada would know what was what with her rational mind and straightforward ways.

Wilma placed small coffee cups on a tray. She'd already made sandwiches for herself and Ada to eat for later, so she put them on a plate, cut off the crusts, and cut them into bite-sized pieces. They could eat them as a snack, along with some of Ada's chocolate cookies, as long as Jared hadn't eaten them all.

Once she'd arranged the coffee and the food onto a large tray, she ventured out to the porch and placed the tray in the center of the tiny table.

After pouring the coffee, she sat opposite Obadiah.

She did her best to act normal, although she was sure something out of the ordinary was happening.

"So, Wilma, tell me about your trip to Cherish's farm." Eli lifted his cup to his lips.

Wilma smiled when she thought about everything that had happened at the farm. So much silliness and excitement always surrounded Cherish. She explained to Obadiah, "Cherish is my youngest daughter."

He nodded.

"It was great. She was delighted with the quilt we made for her, and it was lovely to see Malachi again too. Malachi is her new husband."

"That's nice, and are all your children married now? You have the house to yourself?" Obadiah asked.

"That's right."

"*Jah*, she's all alone. That's why I come here to help as often as possible."

"Not quite."

Both men stared at Wilma.

Then she realized she had to explain the rest of her statement. "I mean going back to your previous question. I don't live alone. Debbie and Krystal live here with Debbie's young son, Jared. Debbie and Krystal aren't my daughters, but they feel like they are sometimes."

Obadiah raised his eyebrows. "Oh, how wonderful. How many children do you have?"

"Six daughters and three stepchildren. Oh, I always forget Bliss," Wilma said with a laugh. "Four stepchildren." Wilma took a bite of her sandwich. She swallowed quickly. "Do you have children, Obadiah?"

Obadiah shook his head in response. "No, I was never blessed with any."

Eli leaned forward. "He never married."

"I see." A curious expression crossed Wilma's face. What a surprise it was to find out Obadiah had remained single. Now she had to know why.

That was a job for Ada.

Where is she? Wilma wondered again. "So, you're just passing through, or do you plan on spending some time here?"

"I'm not sure yet. It depends on a few factors."

"He's had a failed romance and needed to get away." Eli took a bite of his sandwich and was unaware of the slight embarrassment that tinted Obadiah's face.

There *was* a woman around. As much as she expected it, Wilma couldn't help feeling disturbed by the knowledge. He was handsome; it made sense that at least one woman was trying to become his wife.

"He's always been looking for a special someone, but nothing ever panned out," Eli stated.

Wilma shot a glance at Obadiah, who was looking into his coffee. Eli still didn't appear to be aware Obadiah might not have wanted to reveal so much about himself. Wilma chuckled to herself.

"What about you, Wilma? Are you looking for love?" Obadiah asked. It was the last thing Wilma had expected him to say.

Obadiah eased closer to Wilma, setting his cup down on the table. The sudden movement startled her and she stiffened, causing both Eli and Obadiah to turn toward her.

She didn't say anything in response to his question. Where was Ada? She wished desperately for her friend's presence at that moment.

Since Wilma didn't answer Obadiah's question, Eli said, "There will never be anyone else for me except my Frannie. I heard a saying, better to have loved and lost than never to have loved at all." Eli smiled at Wilma and then looked at Obadiah. "Sorry, I shouldn't have said that due to your circumstances."

Obadiah chuckled. "Don't be sorry on my account."

She was glad she didn't answer Obadiah's question. They'd only just reconnected. She couldn't reveal everything about herself. "Eli has been such a blessing since my husband passed away. I'm so thankful for all his help around the orchard. It's so good to have friends."

"I'm so sorry for your loss, Wilma," Obadiah said. "I should've said that before. It must be hard for you. You said you have four stepchildren, so...."

"I was married twice," Wilma said.

It was evident Eli wasn't following what was being said. "I enjoy our conversations, Wilma. I'm grateful for someone who knows what losing someone irreplaceable is like."

Wilma felt a sense of guilt for her feelings for Obadiah. After all, Eli was shackled in his widowhood, desperately keeping his wife's memory alive. In comparison, she was becoming open to the idea of another marriage. After all, she'd never pictured herself growing old alone.

Wilma was trying to think what to say when Obadiah ignored his cousin's comment and asked her a question. "How is your family, Wilma? I remember you have one older sister. Her name escapes me. I'm sorry."

"Thank you for asking," Wilma replied. "Iris passed away a few years ago, so now it's just me with my children and grandchildren."

"I'm so sorry for your loss. Iris was an amazing person."

"She was, and my stepdaughter, Florence, named her first child Iris."

Obadiah nodded. "Iris must've had a big impact on her."

Wilma looked down. There was so much Obadiah didn't know about her. The truth was Florence had never met Iris. Wilma had given the baby she'd had out of wedlock to Iris to raise, then blocked them both from her heart and mind. Wilma regarded her life as a tangled mess, whereas Obadiah's must've been much more straightforward. Would a man such as him accept her past mistakes as well as her failings?

"How is your family?" Wilma asked Obadiah.

"They passed away years ago now. It's only Tiger and me."

"Tiger?"

"Yes, my dog. I take him everywhere with me." He nodded toward the buggy, and Wilma looked over to see a large brown dog with his head out the window, panting.

Wilma's heart dropped. A dog? She knew how people got attached to their dogs, and it seemed Obadiah was that way with his. She could see it in his eyes the way he was looking at the dog. As much as she didn't like pets, dogs included, she wanted Obadiah to like her. "He's a lovely-looking dog."

"Thank you. He's a good boy. Do you like dogs, Wilma?"

"Of course. Who doesn't? I love them." The words had spilled out of her mouth before she could stop them. She'd just lied without hesitation.

"Do you have a dog?" Obadiah asked.

"Cherish had one. She took him with her when she left. We all miss Caramel, and Cherish also had two birds she took with her."

As always, Eli's mind was stuck on Frannie. "It's peculiar how we get accustomed to bereavement at this age." Eli took a sandwich from the plate and bit into it.

"I'll never really get used to it, but who are we to question the Lord's plans?" Wilma took a sip of coffee.

Obadiah smiled at Wilma, and she had to stifle a cough as her coffee went down the wrong way.

Wilma wanted to know so much about Obadiah and his life, but she didn't want to sound like she was interrogating him. "How long are you here for? Oh, sorry, I think I already asked you."

Obadiah smiled. "For as long as I want. I closed up my house, and a neighbor is looking after things until I return."

Wilma sipped her coffee some more, thinking about the relationship Obadiah was trying to recover from. The woman must've lived close to him, and that's why he left. That was well and good, but what would happen when he returned? So often people broke up and got back together. The woman would realize how much she missed him, and they would reunite. No woman would let a man like Obadiah get away from her.

Wilma warned herself not to get too close. The last thing she wanted was another heartbreak due to loss.

As Obadiah talked, Wilma found herself captivated by his voice. It was deep and soothing; she could listen to him for hours. She wondered what it would be like to have him whisper sweet nothings into her ear.

But she quickly shook the thought away. She couldn't afford to indulge in such imaginings. She was a widow, and she had children and grandchildren to think about. She couldn't let herself be distracted by a man who could be in love with someone else.

As they chatted, Wilma's mind kept reverting to the idea of love and companionship. Debbie was marrying Fritz at the end of the year, and Krystal was in love with Jed. It was only a matter of time before those two married and then she'd be alone by herself in her large house.

Maybe she could take a chance on Obadiah if he was truly finished in the relationship with the other woman.

Her thoughts were jolted by Tiger barking loudly from the buggy.

Obadiah apologized and excused himself to tend to his dog. Wilma couldn't help but feel a sense of disappointment as she watched him leave, even if he was coming back in a moment.

It was then she realized she was in trouble.

She felt something for this man.

CHAPTER 2

*C*herish opened her eyes, ready to greet another day. She'd been half awake when Malachi kissed her goodbye before leaving with Simon to work on Simon's house. Immediately Cherish's mind ticked over with a list of chores.

At least she didn't have to do anything alone anymore, not now that Favor was here. With that thought, she jumped out of bed while simultaneously pulling on her bathrobe as she pushed her feet into her fluffy slippers. Then she raced down the hallway to Favor's bedroom door.

"Good morning. What a lovely day." Cherish walked over and pulled aside the curtains allowing the sun to stream through the window. A shaft beamed onto Favor's face causing her to grimace and groan. "There are birds outside. They're so sweet. Don't you just love birds, Favor?"

"What? What's going on?"

Cherish chuckled when she saw the untouched coffee on Favor's nightstand. "Look at that! That's kind. Simon left coffee here for you before you were even awake. I should have Malachi do that for me. What a great idea. I'd call it instant coffee. No wait. Instant coffee is something else and I don't like it. I prefer the drip filter."

Favor sat up. "What time is it? It feels like the middle of the night."

"It's time to wake up, sleepyhead. You never did like mornings. We've got so much to do. Emma and Annie are coming over for breakfast, and then we're taking food to the men at your new house. I'm so excited you're here. We're going to have so much fun."

Favor covered her ears. "Stop talking. Where's my coffee?"

Cherish leaned over and stuck a finger into Favor's coffee. "It's stone cold."

"Why would you do that to my drink?"

Cherish shook the liquid off her finger. "To see if it was warm."

"Obviously, I'm not going to drink it now."

Cherish laughed. "I knew it was cold. I just wanted to know how cold."

"Just get me a hot one, would you?"

"Yes, Ma'am. At your service. Anything else?"

"Breakfast." Favor's head hit the pillow, and she covered her face with the quilt.

"No." Cherish tugged the quilt away. "I'll make you another coffee, but we're waiting for breakfast for when

14

our guests arrive. Did you forget Emma and Annie are coming?"

"No. You just reminded me. How much time do I have to get ready?"

"Enough time. I like to leave myself enough time to do things. I know you're the same. You don't like to rush about at the last minute. Rushing gives me anxiety. How about you?"

"Same."

Cherish took the cold coffee with her and made Favor a piping hot one, and then she sat on her bedside with Favor while she drank it. It didn't matter if Favor was in a bad mood. Her sister was there; nothing could destroy Cherish's optimism for the day ahead. Not only the day ahead, but the years ahead they'd be sharing —together.

After a few minutes, Favor stretched her arms above her head. "Okay, I'm ready to face the day."

Cherish grinned. "That's the way! Now let's get ready for breakfast with our guests."

"Sit and talk for a while," Favor whined.

"Okay. So, are you ready for today?"

"I suppose so," Favor replied, not meeting her gaze. "I just wish I could stay in bed all day, but I know I can't. Not today. Maybe one day soon I can stay in bed all day."

Cherish laughed. "Well, you can't do that anytime soon. We have a busy time ahead of us. The men are working on the house. Aren't you thrilled about that? You'll be living there in no time. Just the two of you."

Favor sighed. "I know, I know. I'm trying to be excited. I am. It's just a lot to take in."

Cherish placed a reassuring hand on Favor's shoulder. "I understand. It's a big change, but it's a good one. We're all here for you, taking it one step at a time. Soon, you'll have everything you ever wanted, and you and Simon will be free from his folks."

"We are free now."

"I know, but it'll be even better when you're in your own home. You'll make your own rules."

Favor grinned. "Yeah. I'll enjoy that. It really is good to be here. I hope things work out for us financially. The last thing I want is for us to go home to Harriet and Melvin because we ran out of money and have to sell the house, the land, and everything."

"Trust me. It will never happen." Cherish couldn't tell her sister she and Malachi were rich. Malachi had kept it a secret for so long, and she agreed it was wise to keep that information to themselves. They would help people where they could, just like how Malachi was assisting young couples in purchasing land for a fraction of the actual value. There was no way Malachi or Cherish would ever let Favor and Simon fail. They'd help them however they could.

It was hard for Cherish to keep a secret, but she was well-practiced at keeping secrets by now. She'd become an excellent secret keeper, but it was challenging to keep good news bottled up.

Cherish stood and walked to the door. "I'm going to start on breakfast now. You better get ready."

"Thanks, Cherish. You're the best."

"I know. Don't you forget it!"

"And don't you forget to get dressed. You can't go around in that old robe all day."

Cherish looked down at her bathrobe. "You're right. I could do with a new one. I'll look in the catalog next time I visit the store."

"I was only joking when I said it was old. Please don't listen to me. New things cost money. I'm sure you've got other things to spend your money on, like feeding your guests," Favor said cheekily.

Cherish shook her head. "The damage is done. I'm buying a new one." With all of Malachi's money, it would be fine if she bought herself a few small items—only things she needed, of course.

"Okay. Do what you want. Just take me with you when you go to the store."

"Sure. We can go everywhere together from now on. Just like the old days."

Favor nodded, and Cherish left the room, closing the door quietly behind her.

Favor lay back, staring at the ceiling while she pondered her next move. She knew she needed to get up and start getting ready for the day, but she couldn't shake off the feeling of unease gnawing at her. It wasn't just the financial worries. It was something else entirely. She couldn't quite put her finger on it. As she lay there, she realized what it was. It was the fact that she was finally starting a new life with Simon, and she didn't know what the future held for them. As much as she disliked living with Simon's parents, it had felt safe.

Favor had always been the type of person who liked to plan everything, but this was something she couldn't plan for. She didn't know what would happen, which scared her. But she knew she couldn't allow fear to hold her back. She had to take a chance and see where this new life would take her and Simon.

With a deep breath, Favor threw off the covers and got out of bed. She walked over to the window and looked out at the beautiful view. The sun was starting to rise over the horizon, casting a warm glow over the landscape. At that moment, a sense of peace washed over her, and she knew everything would be okay.

As she got dressed, she couldn't help but feel grateful for her sister and her husband. They had taken them in and given them a fresh start. They had shown them kindness and love; she knew they would always be there for her and for Simon.

She left her room and headed toward the kitchen, where Cherish was already fully dressed and busily preparing breakfast. The smell of coffee and pancakes filled the air, and Favor's stomach rumbled in anticipation.

"Did Malachi and Simon eat before they left this morning?" Favor asked.

"From what was left in the sink, it looked like they had peanut butter and honey toast."

Favor laughed. "That's a strange combination, but Simon likes it."

"That's funny, so does Malachi. They're going to get along great."

Just then, they heard a horse and buggy.

"That'll be them now." Favor rushed to the door and opened it for Annie and Emma, who'd arrived in the same buggy.

"I hope they're hungry," Cherish said as she turned to the food on the stove.

Cherish carefully arranged a warm plate of fluffy golden-yellow pancakes and piled them onto a platter in the middle of her dining table. Next to them lay the bacon, waffles, and fresh butter.

The women came into the house and greeted Cherish.

"Wow, this looks amazing!" exclaimed Annie as they all sat down to eat.

"Yes, I'm starving," said Emma. "I apologize for not being here to help prepare breakfast this morning."

Cherish shook her head. "There's no need for that."

After their silent prayers of thanks for their food, they started filling their plates with food.

Between munching on a waffle, Favor said, "I'm so thrilled to be back in this lovely community and away from Simon's parents." She still couldn't believe how lucky she was to be there finally.

"It's great to have you here, Favor!" Annie chirped. "You've told us about his parents before. Are they really that bad?"

Favor covered her mouth. "Oh no. I didn't remember I'd told you before."

Cherish helped her out. "Simon's parents are devoted to him. He's the only son."

"Only child," Favor added. "I don't think his mother can live without him. That's how she acts. Anyway, we've got a break from them for now."

"Everything we discussed when you were here has come true!" Emma enthused.

"Except for the baby part," Annie added.

"Don't worry. There's still hope for that!" Favor replied. "We can still all have babies that will grow up with each other. Although, I would've liked to have had a baby by now. I'm getting older and don't want to be an old mother. I want to have great-grandchildren when I'm old. If I wait too long, I'll die before that happens. But I keep reminding myself it'll happen if God wills it."

Cherish smiled at Favor and added enthusiastically, "I'm sure it'll happen. I can't wait for our kids to grow up together!"

"I hope and pray that's what happens. Imagine if all four of us got pregnant at the same time. Our children would be like quads," Emma said.

Everyone laughed at that thought, and Annie added a few funny comments.

As the group of friends continued their conversation, Favor's thoughts drifted to her struggles with fertility. She had been trying to conceive for years but with no success. Every month, she would pray for a positive pregnancy test, but it never came. She had tried everything from tracking her ovulation to taking special herbs suggested to work, but still nothing.

Harriet and Melvin had to be disappointed in her. They would be hoping and praying too that they could have another little Simon or a Simone to dote on.

Favor sat listening to her friends talk about their future children. She couldn't help but feel a tinge of sadness. Why did she have to struggle so much? First, it was getting away from Simon's parents, and now that made her childless state loom larger.

They had a house, so they had to fill it with children. Her heart ached with longing for a child of her own. Favor pushed those thoughts aside and forced a smile. She wanted to maintain the mood of the conversation so she joined in with the laughter and the jokes as though she didn't have a single care in the world.

Cherish was delighted she had a group of friends to fill her life with happiness. She looked over at the smile on Favor's face, and her heart was even fuller.

Finally, Cherish felt content with her circumstances. After months of concern over Malachi's mysterious financial situation on the farm, she discovered they were wealthier than she'd ever imagined. There was no danger of them losing the property. Every day brought her more peace, and she was less nostalgic for the home at the Baker Apple Orchard.

"How did you manage to escape from Simon's parents?" Annie questioned Favor.

Favor rolled her eyes before responding. "Let me tell you, it was no easy feat."

"Will they be visiting soon?" Cherish inquired.

Favor's eyes widened. "Frankly, it wouldn't surprise me if they came tomorrow."

Cherish gave Favor a stern look of disapproval.

"What?" Favor questioned.

"Do you think they'd do that?" Cherish asked.

"Do you think they wouldn't?" Favor countered, meeting Cherish's gaze head-on.

"You're right. Anything is possible with them," Cherish conceded.

The women chuckled at the situation.

"I suppose meeting them will be an experience," Emma said.

"Oh, believe me, the novelty wears off fast!" When the room fell silent, Favor felt a twinge of guilt for talking negatively about Simon's parents, but she knew the words wouldn't go any further than that room. She could trust these women.

Once they were finished breakfast, the women decided to rest before beginning their lunch preparations for the men. Annie put on some tea for them and sat in the kitchen, keeping Cherish company as she put away the dishes from earlier. Emma and Favor caught up in Cherish's living room, chatting away.

"So, I would like you to give me more advice on alpacas, Emma. We have yet to decide what kind of farm to have. Jed mentioned something about pigeons. He thought it could be a great way to make some money."

Emma shook her head. "I have no idea," she replied. "But there is a huge interest in alpaca products. Zeke and I are doing exceptionally well this season because our farm is the only one nearby, and people from the city love it. We've been talking about expanding. Maybe we should consider talking about it with Simon and Zeke. There may be a way to join us and sell more products, then divide our profits. There could be a deal that benefits everyone."

Favor smiled. "Would you do that for us?"

"Of course. We can show you how it's done. However, we'd have to get approval from the men first."

"That would be great!" exclaimed Favor. "We could do pigeons as well. Jed said they don't take up a lot of space."

"Maybe if that's what you want to do."

"We'll do anything if it makes financial sense."

Emma chuckled. "It's obvious you're looking forward to life here. I can hear it in your voice."

Favor nodded eagerly. "I've been imagining this day for ages, ever since I got married."

Cherish and Annie strode into the room, and Annie placed the tea and freshly baked cookies on the table in the center of the living room before slumping into one of the nearby chairs.

"We've just had breakfast. How can we eat all this?" Emma asked.

Cherish chuckled. "Just have the tea then. We need the energy to face the day. I'm so glad everyone's here. This is so much better than being alone," Cherish declared before she returned to sipping her hot tea.

Then she looked over at Annie. "Annie, what's wrong? You're not your usual self today."

Favor cast a concerned glance at Annie. Favor had been so caught up in her problems she hadn't noticed something was wrong with her new friend.

"Uh," Annie muttered.

"You don't have to tell us if you don't want to," Cherish said, placing a reassuring hand on Annie's shoulder.

Annie smiled at Cherish before continuing. "Well, Gus's parents are thinking about buying the general store, and then Gus and I would be working there."

Favor tilted her head to one side. "But you don't want to do that?"

Favor furrowed her brow, but then she noticed Cherish giving her a look telling her not to press Annie too much.

"Yes, let's leave this subject for now; nothing is certain yet, so please keep it quiet," Annie requested. "It's probably too early for me to have said anything."

The others all nodded in agreement. "Of course," Emma replied.

Favor thought about whether Annie had in-laws like hers, causing her to feel guilty for making her dislike of them so evident in front of Annie, who was smiling politely and saying nothing about her own family.

She couldn't help but wonder if Simon would be better off with someone like Annie, someone able to keep quiet and put up with whatever Harriet and Melvin threw their way. Perhaps Favor was too strong-minded and hard-headed to ever fit into their family dynamic. Favor tried to put her worries out of her mind. It was all irrelevant now that they were far removed from their old lives where Harriet ruled the roost.

They all got into Annie's buggy a little later and headed to Favor's new house. Favor sat in the back with Cherish. All the while, she couldn't help but feel a sense of excitement mixed with nervousness. This was it, the start of her new life.

As they bumped along the dirt road, Cherish turned to her. "Are you okay? You seem a bit quiet."

Favor nodded. "Yeah, I'm just taking it all in. It's a lot to process, you know?"

"I know. But you're going to be just fine. And Simon too. This will be the start of a wonderful new chapter in your lives."

Favor smiled. "I believe that. And I'm so grateful for you and Malachi. I don't know what we would have done without you."

Cherish placed a hand on her arm. "You don't have to thank us. We're family. We take care of each other."

Favor nodded, feeling a lump form in her throat. She didn't want to cry, but the emotions were over-whelming. She was starting a new life with Simon in their own home.

As they approached the house, Favor's heart raced. It was a modest home, but it was hers. She couldn't wait to see what it would be like when the men finished it.

Favor looked around. She saw the rolling hills and noticed a small pond in the distance. She couldn't believe this was all hers. When she looked back at the house, it looked so bare. It needed a garden and perhaps a couple of trees nearby. "It's so beautiful, Cherish. Thank you for getting this organized for us." She noticed Malachi walking up to them. "Thank you too, Malachi."

"You don't have to keep thanking us," Cherish told her.

"Are you ready to see our progress?" Malachi asked, a twinkle in his eye.

Favor nodded eagerly, and they all walked toward the house. As they entered, Favor was surprised at how much work had already been done. The holes in the walls were gone, the floors had been sanded, and a couple of rotting boards had been replaced. It was starting to look like a real home.

CHAPTER 3

One by one, Favor's new friends carried plates of food into her kitchen.

Cherish looked around to see a completely new kitchen had been installed in their absence. She turned around to see Favor's face, hoping she liked gray because the countertops, drawers, and cupboards were all the same mid-toned gray.

"Do you like it?" Cherish asked with a certain degree of hesitation.

"I love it! I love everything. I still can't believe this house is ours. The kitchen looks brand new. I don't know where they managed to find it."

"Malachi knows someone who works in a salvage yard. It does look brand new. It's unbelievable what people get rid of."

Favor looked in every room of her new home, appreciating the compliments from her friends even though she knew they were just being polite. To them, it was just four walls and a roof, but to her, it was a refuge.

She was relieved to be away from Simon's parents and loved her little house no matter what it looked like. She'd make it so pretty when the repairs were complete. They would eventually get furniture and they'd throw a few soft cushions on the couch, and then a painting on the wall would make all the difference.

Meanwhile, Cherish was still fixated on the kitchen. "Are you sure you like the kitchen? You didn't choose it."

"I love it."

"Are you sure?" Cherish queried in a hushed tone as she moved closer to Favor. "Are you angry you weren't informed about it? I didn't even know about it."

Favor chuckled and gave Cherish a playful shove on the shoulder. "It's better than living with Simon's parents for the rest of my life. It's fine. I told you I love everything, and I mean it."

Cherish was amazed to see how much had changed in Favor's attitude.

"Don't forget I get to pick the paint colors, right? We have a roof over our heads that Harriet and Melvin don't own."

Cherish grew concerned that Favor was still negatively speaking about Harriet and Melvin. She didn't want the others to think Favor wasn't kind. Favor's personality could only be understood if someone fully knew her.

When they went back to make a second trip to the buggy to fetch more food, Cherish took hold of Favor's arm. "Hey."

She stopped. "What is it?"

"You're making a lot of comments about Harriet and Melvin. I wouldn't want people to think you're being unkind or gossiping."

Favor crossed her arms in front of her. "Did someone say something? Who was it?"

"No one."

"Was it Emma, or was it Annie? Because if it was Emma, I wouldn't be happy living next door to her."

"No. They're not like that. No one said anything. I want them to see the real you."

"This is the real me."

"I want you to focus on building a happy life with Simon without dwelling in the past or carrying ill feelings toward Simon's folks."

"Okay, you're right. We are so blessed to be here finally. Thanks, Cherish. I'll make sure I'm careful what I say. I'll only say bad things about them in front of you."

Cherish laughed, wondering if Favor was serious or not. Either way, she was relieved the conversation didn't take a wrong turn. "Let's get this food served up for the men."

Once the men were in the kitchen for lunch, they gathered in a circle, eating and talking. Suddenly Jed walked into the room.

"Jed," Cherish said. "I wasn't aware you were helping out."

"Of course I am. What else would I be doing? Weren't you there when Malachi asked me?"

Cherish shrugged her shoulders. "I don't remember."

"Thank you for assisting us with the house. I appreciate it," Favor told Jed.

"Anything for family," Jed replied with a playful wink before heading to get himself something to eat.

When he was out of earshot, Cherish leaned closer to Favor and said, "Krystal and Jed are in love."

"Really?" Favor asked, surprised. "She stopped at Harriet and Melvin's farm on the way back but didn't tell me about him. I sensed something different about her, and she told me she'd tell me later. That must've been it."

Cherish nodded. "I think they make a good couple."

"What happened with Matthew?"

Cherish's eyes widened. "It's a long story, but in a nutshell, she wanted to check if he'd be faithful, so she put him to the test with someone else. He fell for it."

Favor couldn't believe what she was hearing. Her jaw dropped wide open.

"Yes, and it gets even worse," Cherish began. "The girl Krystal set him up with also fell for him."

Favor gasped in shock and put a hand over her heart. "Oh no! I had no idea. That must be heartbreaking for Krystal."

"I know. She's had a really tough time with

Matthew. I don't think he's good for her. He also dumped her for Fenella as well."

"The last thing she deserves is more pain." As her closest confidant in the community, Favor felt compelled to help Krystal find someone who could make her happy.

"Jed's a bit strange, but he's good-hearted."

"What do you mean?" asked Favor.

"He's got his own ideas about things. He disregards the rules. He doesn't care that Krystal was born an *Englisher,* though."

"That's a good thing, right?"

"Of course. I think he makes her feel comfortable being herself. He's been moping around, acting depressed since she left."

"I thought he seemed a bit short with you."

"That's just Jed. He doesn't mean anything by it. It's just how he comes across."

Favor gave a nod. "I'll try to remember that."

After lunch, the men returned to work on the repairs while Cherish and Favor stayed behind to clean the kitchen. Cherish wanted to talk more about Krystal, but she could sense Favor was preoccupied with something else.

"Is everything okay, Favor?" Cherish asked, noticing the worry lines etched on her sister's face.

"I can't stop thinking about Krystal," Favor admitted. "She joined the community because of me. I need to do something to help her."

"Like what?"

"I don't know yet. Maybe I could talk to her and see how she's doing."

"That's a good idea. I'm sure she would appreciate that."

Favor nodded. "I just want her to be happy, you know? She deserves it after everything she's been through."

"I know. And maybe Jed could be the one to make her happy."

Favor smiled. "You like him, don't you?"

Cherish stopped what she was doing and thought about the question momentarily. "Well, he seems like a good match for Krystal. And he's Malachi's brother, which makes him family now, so I want him to be happy too."

Favor chuckled. "I suppose you're right. We'll have to see if we can do anything to help them along the path to marital bliss."

They both put their heads together and laughed. It was like they were children again, plotting their next scheme to annoy Florence or their mother. This time, though, their scheme would be more beneficial.

As they finished cleaning the kitchen, Favor's mind continued to bubble over with ideas of how she could help Krystal.

It would be challenging with so many miles between Krystal and Jed, but Cherish and she were determined to help Krystal find happiness.

CHAPTER 4

*A*fter Obadiah and Eli left, Wilma moved the clothes that were waiting to be washed so she could sit on the couch. She looked up at the ceiling and tried to talk sense into herself.

She was giddy, like a young woman in love for the first time. But being in the late range of middle-aged, she was no spring chicken. As she sat there, lost in thought, she couldn't help but replay the scene with Obadiah in her mind. His rugged good looks and muscular build made her heart race, but it wasn't merely his appearance that drew her in. It was the way he spoke to her and the things he said.

Her marriage to Levi had been one of a deep friendship that had developed into love as the years passed.

Josiah, her first husband and the father of her six girls had been her one true love, but he was gone, and her memory of him had faded with the passing of the years.

She stood up and walked to the window, looking for Ada. Ada would probably tell her she was an old fool to have such thoughts.

Or would she tell her to go for it? Ada was always saying Eli would've been a good match only he couldn't keep quiet about Frannie for even five minutes.

It was odd to entertain thoughts of a third marriage, but she couldn't help it.

It was a while before Wilma realized a horse and buggy was coming up the driveway. When she spotted it, she quickly composed herself and went to greet Ada and Samuel.

Ada had one foot out of the buggy when Wilma reached her.

Ada froze, looking down at her. "What's wrong?"

"Nothing's wrong." Wilma glanced over at Samuel. He always drove Ada to the house because Ada didn't like to drive a buggy. "Morning, Samuel."

"Good morning, but it's almost afternoon." He gave a good-natured chuckle.

"Yes. It could be afternoon by now. Why are you so late?" Wilma blurted out.

As Ada closed the buggy door, she laughed. "I didn't know I had a schedule to keep."

"You don't. It's just you're usually here earlier than this."

Ada waved to Samuel, who turned the buggy around before heading back down the long driveway.

Ada turned to Wilma. "What is it? Are you ill?"

Wilma took her best friend's arm and walked with her to the house. "Eli brought his cousin here."

"Obadiah?"

Wilma stopped still and stared at her friend. "Yes. How did you know they were cousins?"

"I ran into them yesterday at the store."

"They were just here, and now they've gone. I hoped you'd come. I didn't know what to say."

"You always know what to say. Why are you acting odd?"

Wilma swallowed hard and then continued toward the house. "I'm not."

"Yes, you are."

Wilma pushed the front door open, and Ada followed Wilma into the kitchen.

"I know what's going on. Do you think Obadiah's going to be your third husband? Really, Wilma? You don't know anything about the man. He's had a lifetime away from here. At least with Eli, you know everything he's been through. I mean, Obadiah might have been involved in… anything."

Wilma was speechless. How could Ada possibly know what she'd been thinking? It was uncanny, but they had been best friends for most of their lives, so it made sense from that viewpoint.

Wilma sat down at the kitchen table, and Ada sat opposite. "I don't want to marry Eli or Obadiah. I'll make that clear."

"I thought Eli liked you as more than a friend, but

35

now I'm not sure. If Eli were serious about finding a wife, he'd have to stop talking about his late wife for one minute."

"Oh, Ada, he doesn't talk about her that much."

"It's nice how he keeps her memory alive, though. I wonder if Samuel would do the same for me?" Ada bit her lip as she pondered the thought.

Wilma was flustered by Ada's ability to read her thoughts so easily, but she tried not to show it. She wasn't ready to fully confide in her friend just yet. "Tea?"

"You know the answer."

Wilma smiled and got up to make them a pot of tea. As Wilma turned on the stove and filled the kettle with water, she couldn't help but let her mind wander back to Obadiah. Ada was right; she knew nothing about him, but he intrigued her.

Maybe it was how he carried himself or how his eyes seemed to light up when he talked about old times. Whatever it was, Wilma felt drawn to him in a way she couldn't explain.

After the water boiled, Wilma poured the water into the teapot and added a few tea bags. She brought the pot and two cups to the table and waited for the teabags to permeate into the water, trying her best to act casual.

"So, what do you think of Obadiah?" Ada picked up the teapot and swirled it around.

"He seems nice enough, I suppose. But as you said,

we don't really know him now. I found out he's never been married. Can you imagine that at his age? I think he's here to have some space from this woman, whoever she is." Wilma shrugged and hoped Ada could offer some insight. She could've heard something more about Obadiah and this woman, and knowing Ada, she would share the information.

Ada then poured the tea into two cups. "He could be trying to win her back."

Wilma wasn't pleased with that idea. "How would he be winning her back from here?"

"Absence makes the heart grow fonder, they say. It could be a ploy." Ada took a sip of tea.

Wilma raised an eyebrow.

Ada set her teacup down on the saucer. "It sounds to me like there are some things to know about that relationship. That is, if you're interested in him."

Wilma laughed nervously. "Eli just mentioned the failed romance briefly. I'm only bringing it up to… to keep you informed."

"We certainly don't want any more drama around here." Ada stared at Wilma.

Wilma nodded in agreement, but her mind drifted off to Obadiah once again. What was he doing right now, and what he was thinking? Suddenly, Ada's voice broke her train of thought.

"You seem distracted, Wilma. Are you sure everything is okay?"

"Yes, sorry. I have a lot on my mind. I mean,

Florence is having the baby soon. Then we have Miriam and Earl having their twins. I'll have to mail them some gifts because I don't want to visit them yet. It's such a long way to go. Then we have Debbie's wedding to plan. So much to do."

Ada gave her a knowing look. "I think you're in love, Wilma. Admit it."

Wilma blushed. "I don't know what you're talking about."

Ada chuckled. "It's okay, Wilma. You're allowed to have a crush. Just be careful. We don't know anything about him, and you don't want to get hurt. Eli would've been better for you because we know him well."

"I won't get hurt." There was no use denying it, not when Ada could see into her mind as easily as reading the pages of a book.

Ada nodded, but her face was a mask of skepticism. "Just be careful. That's all I'm saying."

"I will."

The two women sipped their tea silently for a few minutes before Ada spoke up again. "You know, there's something about Obadiah that makes me uneasy. I can't put my finger on it."

Wilma looked at her friend with concern. "What do you mean?"

"I don't know. It's just a feeling. There's something about him that doesn't sit right with me."

Wilma took another sip of her tea, thinking about what Ada might be picking up. She certainly hadn't felt anything bad surrounding Obadiah. She didn't want to dismiss Ada's concerns, but at the same time, she didn't want to give up her attraction to Obadiah. It was nice to have a special someone to think about. "Maybe it's just because he's like a stranger now. We're not used to having outsiders come into our community. Even though we know him, you might feel like you don't because we haven't seen him in several years."

Ada nodded slowly. "Maybe that's all it is. I've always said it's easy for the young to find love. It's much harder to make those kinds of connections when you're older."

Wilma took her friend's words to heart. She knew Ada was right but couldn't help how she felt. The road to love at her age wasn't easy, but it could be worth it if everything worked out.

"Don't listen to me. I guess you're never too old for love." Ada chuckled. "I'm just glad I don't have to concern myself with it."

Wilma smiled. "You don't have to concern yourself with love? Hmm. How does Samuel feel about that?"

Ada shook her finger at Wilma, scolding her playfully. "You know what I mean. I don't need the thrill of a new love because I have a long-lasting love with Samuel."

Wilma let out a sigh and looked at Ada with envy. She had never experienced a long-lasting love like the one Ada and Samuel shared. Wilma had always longed for the comfort of a long-lasting love, but it was never going to be. At her age, that ship had left the port.

Before Ada and Wilma had realized it, their day

together was over. Tonight, Ada and Samuel weren't staying for the evening meal.

Wilma accompanied Ada to their buggy, where the ever-patient Samuel waited. Then she stood alone and watched as they drove away.

When they were out of sight, she stayed still, feeling something profound was about to happen. She couldn't explain what it was.

As the sun began to set and the sky changed to shades of pink and orange, Wilma decided to take a walk before everyone came home. She needed to clear her head and get some fresh air before preparing the evening meal.

When she was in the midst of the orchard between the rows of apple trees, she couldn't shake the feeling she was being watched. She turned around, but no one was there. She continued walking, but the feeling persisted. When she quickened her pace, the sensation grew stronger.

When she saw something move out of the corner of her eye, she froze. The only thing that would be moving was a person. No worker would be in the orchard at sunset. Was she in danger? She whipped her head around to see an orange dog staring at her.

After a dog had bitten her when she was a young child, she'd always avoided dogs. The fear was still there. The dog didn't move, and neither did she, yet their eyes locked.

"Shoo!" Wilma said in a voice that even frightened her. The dog scampered away.

As Wilma returned to her house, she was relieved the dog hadn't attacked her. It could've had rabies or some other frightful disease. The feeling of being watched hadn't left her. It was as if someone was following her, taking in her every move. She quickened her pace some more, looking around nervously.

When she neared the house, she was delighted to see Krystal's horse and buggy coming up the driveway. She was no longer alone.

Krystal stepped out of the buggy and approached Wilma, concern etched on her face. "Wilma, are you okay? You look troubled."

Wilma took a deep breath, trying to compose herself. "I'm fine. I just had a strange feeling someone was following me. Then I saw a dog, and it must've just been that."

"What dog?"

"An unsightly dog with orange fur sticking up. It might be a stray." Wilma shook her head, thinking how awful the animal looked.

"Oh, the poor thing. Was it hungry?"

Wilma felt bad. She didn't even think of that. "I'm not sure."

"I've never seen a dog in the orchard. I'll ask around about it. I'll check with Fairfax tomorrow. He'll want to know if there's a stray in the orchard."

"Thank you, Krystal. You're very kind."

Krystal laughed. "It's not a big deal."

Wilma smiled. "I'll make a start on the meal. We're

having heated-up leftovers tonight. I hope that's all right."

"Sounds great to me."

Wilma headed to the house while Krystal set about unhitching the buggy.

CHAPTER 5

*W*ilma was up early, alone in her kitchen, cooking breakfast while waiting for Ada to arrive. Krystal had left for work, and Debbie and Jared had also gone.

It was a cold and crisp morning, and Wilma was grateful for the warmth emanating from the stove. She watched the bacon sizzle in the frying pan as it filled the kitchen with the mouth-watering scent of pork. As she flipped the bacon, she heard a knock at the door.

Wilma jumped. This couldn't be Ada; she never knocked.

Wilma turned off the stove and tied off her apron before opening the front door.

Obadiah stood, clutching a colorful bunch of flowers.

It was a delightful and yet unexpected sight. A fluttering sensation churned Wilma's insides at the sight of the man before her. "Obadiah! I didn't expect you."

"I apologize for dropping by unannounced like this. I was taking a stroll and thought of you when I saw these flowers, so I brought them to you."

"Thank you. They're lovely. Please come inside."

As Wilma took the flowers from him, his sleeve drew up, and she saw an unsightly scar. He quickly pulled down his sleeve, and Wilma pretended she hadn't noticed.

Wilma showed him into the kitchen, and she stooped down in the cupboard and pulled out a vase. After she filled it up with water, she arranged the flowers carefully and then set the vase in the center of the table.

What was the scar from? She wanted to ask but felt she shouldn't.

"They're so pretty. Thank you for these. Flowers do brighten up a room." When she turned around, he'd already sat at the kitchen table.

"The bacon sure smells good," he said.

"It does. We should go into the living room. You don't need to see the mess in here." Wilma gave a little laugh.

"It's fine. Besides, you and I must have a different opinion of what a mess is. It looks very tidy here. Did I show up at an inconvenient moment?"

"Not at all. I'm just waiting for Ada. I was just about to eat breakfast. Would you like some? I cooked breakfast once already for the others, but sometimes I don't eat with them. I eat alone when it's quiet or with Ada when she gets here. Oh, I don't mean I wouldn't rather eat with you." She put a hand to her head, worried about what she'd said.

He chuckled. "You'd rather eat by yourself?"

"No. Not at all. Sometimes Ada comes, and I eat with her, but she's not here yet."

"Ada Berger?"

"Yes. Do you remember her?"

"Of course, I remember Ada and Samuel too. I ran into them a couple of days ago. But I remember each of them from before they were married, and then they visited my community a few years ago."

Wilma was slightly disappointed to learn Obadiah had a good memory and recalled Ada; it wasn't just her he remembered. Did that mean she wasn't as important to him as she might have hoped? "Yes, they used to travel a lot. They don't do so much anymore. Ada's been to Cherish's farm several times, and that's the only traveling she's done. Samuel stays at home."

"She doesn't go to the farm with Samuel?"

"She did once, but Samuel doesn't mind staying home while Ada keeps me company."

"It's good to have a close friend."

"Would you care for some eggs? I could scramble some eggs, and we could have them with the bacon if you haven't eaten."

"I'm fine, thank you."

Wilma stared at him, wondering if he was merely being polite. "Have you eaten?"

"No, but..."

"In that case, you need a decent breakfast. Some say it's the most important meal of the day?"

He gave her a big smile. "Thank you. In that case, I won't say no."

"Coffee or hot tea?"

"Coffee, please. I don't drink much tea."

"I only drink it when Ada's here. She likes tea. And it's easier to have that than make tea and coffee. Oh, where's Tiger?" Wilma was sure he'd appreciate her mentioning his dog. After all, he'd like her more if she liked his pet. "Maybe he'd like something to eat too?"

He shook his head. "Tiger's fine. He likes to curl up in the buggy when I'm visiting."

"Okay, but he might change his mind if he gets a whiff of the bacon."

Obadiah chuckled softly.

Before long, Wilma placed the warm plate on the table when the meal was prepared. Obadiah smiled at the plate in front of him.

"It looks and smells wonderful," he said as Wilma poured him a cup of coffee.

Wilma sat beside him, feeling a special joy to be cooking for a man once again. They both closed their eyes in a moment of gratitude, the words of their silent prayer still lingering in their heads when they heard an exuberant voice.

"Yoo-Hoo!"

Ada's loud call made Wilma jump causing her to spill some of her coffee onto the table. "Oh no, I'm so sorry," Wilma mumbled as she quickly ran to grab a dishcloth.

Obadiah rose to his feet as Ada entered the room.

"Oh, hello! I didn't expect anyone else here this morning." Ada observed the freshly picked flowers that now sat in the center of the table.

Obadiah extended his hand, saying warmly, "Ada, it's wonderful to see you again."

Ada examined him closely and then shook his hand.

"Oh, my goodness! What a pleasant surprise to see you here, Obadiah. Wilma, why didn't you say Obadiah would be here for breakfast?" As Ada focused on Wilma, she realized her friend was frazzled as she hastily wiped down the table with a rag.

"It must have slipped my mind. I mean, I didn't know myself."

"I surprised her," Obadiah said.

Wilma walked to the sink and left the rag there before sitting with Ada and Obadiah. Ada was seated next to Wilma, with her gaze resting upon Obadiah.

"What can I get you, Ada?" Wilma asked.

"Nothing. I'm fine, thank you."

"So, what brings you to town?" Ada asked Obadiah as she stole a piece of toast from Wilma's plate.

"I have some unfinished business I never had the opportunity to complete," Obadiah replied with a smile directed toward Wilma, who blushed and shifted in her seat.

Ada noticed Wilma's odd mannerisms and frowned

slightly. "Are you married, Obadiah? Do you have children? We have so much to catch up on."

Wilma stared down at the table. She'd already told Ada all this information.

He set down his knife and fork and rubbed his chin. "Sadly, I never had the chance to have a family. I've never married, so children have remained an unfulfilled hope."

Ada gasped in shock. "That must be horrible! I'm so sorry. Children do give one a sense of purpose. Although, I haven't seen mine for a while. They say they'll visit us soon, but it never seems to happen. They are busy."

Obadiah smiled and then took a mouthful of coffee. "It's fine. Overall, my life turned out quite well. Other than the missing spouse and children, of course."

Wilma liked that he could make light of something that must've been hard for him. He seemed good-natured, and that's just how she remembered him.

"Are you trying to find someone here?" Ada queried "It's not too late, or do you feel it's too late for you? Men can have children when they're old if you find a young wife."

Wilma couldn't help being annoyed by Ada's comment. She didn't want Obadiah to find a young wife. She wanted to explore the possibility of getting to know Obadiah better.

"Everyone's different, they tell me. It depends on what you want for your future." Ada took a large bite out of Wilma's buttered toast.

Obadiah let out another chuckle, and Wilma felt uncomfortable listening to Ada interrogate Obadiah.

"If it's meant to be, it will happen. It's all in *Gott's* hands." Obadiah took up his knife and fork, his gaze briefly locking with Wilma's.

"Wilma, why are you so quiet? Are you okay?" Ada asked as Wilma's face reddened.

"I'm alright," she replied. "I haven't fully recovered from our trip. I'm just a bit tired."

Obadiah nodded. "That's normal for our age."

"Maybe for you two, it's normal," Ada commented, "but I'm always full of energy."

"It's true," Wilma agreed. "Ada is always brimming with energy. She likes to get in and get things done."

"You're still the same, Ada. You haven't changed one bit." Obadiah chuckled.

Ada joined in his laughter. "I'm impressed you remember. They say elephants have long memories, so you're not alone."

"My memory is excellent," he said, pulling back his shoulders. "And I'm not even an elephant."

Ada smiled. "Wilma has a good memory, too," Ada added, glancing at Wilma, who blushed again in response. "Wilma remembers many things from child-hood and when she was a teenager."

As the conversation lulled, the three continued eating their breakfast silently. Wilma kept stealing glances at Obadiah, feeling her heart flutter with admiration for the man across from her.

Ada noticed the silent communication between

them and couldn't help feeling protective. She wanted Wilma to be happy, but they knew nothing about who this man had become. She hadn't had enough time to ask around about him, but that was something she fully intended to do. While she was doing that, she needed Wilma to also get some information from him. Then she'd see if Wilma's information matched the facts that Ada would find out about him. If not, that meant Obadiah had something to hide.

"Wilma, I have a proposition for you," Ada said, staring intently at her best friend.

"What kind of proposition?" Wilma asked, her curiosity piqued.

"I have a friend who's visiting from out of town. He's looking for a tour guide to show him around. I thought you'd be perfect for the job."

Wilma's heart sank. She wasn't sure she was ready to take on such a responsibility, and she wanted to be available for Obadiah while he was around. "I'm not sure I have the time," she said hesitantly.

"It's just for a few hours," Ada insisted.

"I suppose I could spare a little time."

"Good." Ada turned to Obadiah. "I've just arranged a tour guide for you."

He raised his eyebrows. "Wilma?"

"Yes."

Obadiah frowned. "I'm not sure I need that. I grew up here."

Now Wilma was even more embarrassed. "I'm sure Obadiah knows the town he grew up in. It hasn't changed that much. I didn't know you were talking about Obadiah."

"I know you didn't know because you would've said yes immediately." Ada reached for the last piece of toast from Wilma's plate.

Obadiah cleared his throat. "I'm free tomorrow, Wilma. Or the day after if you have some time."

"To show you around your hometown?" Wilma asked him.

"Sure. I said I had a good memory, but it's not good for places. I was talking about having a memory for people and faces, not places."

Ada chuckled to herself. "Places, not faces," she mimicked.

"I'd be delighted to show you around in that case. Shall I pick you up from Eli's house at about nine in the morning?"

"No. I'll come to you. I can be here at nine."

"Perfect." Ada dusted toast crumbs from her fingers.

Wilma was excited about the opportunity to spend more time with him. Although, she didn't like the way Ada embarrassed her.

After they finished breakfast, Obadiah stood up and adjusted his coat. "Thank you for the lovely meal, Wilma." Obadiah caught Wilma's hand in his as they stood up from the table. "Thank you for agreeing to show me around, Wilma. I'm looking forward to tomorrow."

Wilma felt her cheeks flush at his touch. "It's my pleasure, Obadiah."

Obadiah turned to Ada. "And thank you, Ada, for arranging everything."

Ada grinned mischievously. "Don't thank me yet. You haven't seen Wilma's version of a tour yet. That'll be interesting."

Obadiah chuckled. "I'm sure I'll be fully entertained."

Once Obadiah had left, Wilma and Ada found themselves in the kitchen doing the dishes from breakfast. Ada eyed Wilma curiously, her brows knitting together. "What was wrong with you this morning? You were acting weird."

"I was acting weird? What about you? You were saying some strange things," Wilma said.

"I had to say what I said because it was all in response to how you were behaving."

Wilma frowned. "How was I behaving?"

"Wrong word choice. I meant how you were—your demeanor."

Wilma realized there was no way to keep any secrets from Ada, who would relentlessly ask questions until she got her desired answers. So, Wilma chose the path of least resistance and opted for honesty. She threw her tea towel over her shoulder and spun around to meet Ada's gaze. Ada had been washing dishes next to Wilma but paused when Wilma started speaking again. "Was it that obvious?" Wilma asked.

"I know you better than you know yourself." Ada chuckled.

"Oh, Ada. He was the first man I ever loved. I never

dreamed I'd meet him again one day. Even if our paths crossed, nothing else could happen - we're way too old to initiate a romance. We can't turn back the clock."

"No, you can't, but why must you do that?"

Wilma sighed. "Every now and again, I did wonder what had become of him. No one ever mentioned him or his family, and I never asked."

"I never knew."

"It was not something to talk about. It was just something in the back of my mind. Should I make the most of this chance, or am I too old?"

"You're old, but you're not dead. You're still alive, and I'm almost sure he likes you, so why wouldn't you take hold of this chance? If he didn't like you, why was he here today? Take hold of this opportunity *Gott* has given you. Take hold with both hands."

That confirmed Wilma's feelings, and she was glad to hear it. "What makes you so sure he likes me?"

"He kept glancing in your direction with a big grin. And, if I'm correct, I'm guessing he brought you those flowers."

Wilma couldn't keep the smile from her face when she looked at the vase of flowers. "The flowers don't mean anything. He was just being nice."

"Yes, but it seemed like he had to look at you and smile after every response he gave me."

"I don't know, Ada. I think he smiles at everybody. He has always been like that."

"I'm always right, Wilma. And besides, what do you have to lose? Having said that, I have to water down what I said with a good dose of caution and a dollop of awareness. Don't be blind to red flags, and don't rush in. Get to know him fully. I'll see what I can find out from my friends."

"No, don't do that, Ada."

"I must. We need to know about him. He won't tell us if there's something bad, but my friends will. I have friends in every community you can name. If there's anything to know, someone will know something."

Wilma shook her head. "Don't do it. What would happen if he found out we were asking about him? He'd be offended and blame me for being untrusting."

"He won't find out a thing. Besides, it'll be me doing the asking, not you. We both want this to work. I want you to be happy, and Samuel needs some male friends. It was so convenient Levi and Samuel were so close. Samuel needs another best friend."

Wilma shook her head. "I'm being unpractical. I don't need to lose another husband. I can't go through that again."

"Well, this time, things might be different."

Wilma's eyebrows pinched together. "How so?"

"If you marry Obadiah, you might die before him."

Wilma's lips turned down. "Well, thanks for that thought. That's a lovely image to have in my head."

Ada chuckled. "Live for the day, Wilma. Don't stop yourself from being happy because of something that may or may not happen in the future. Having said that, you must wait until I find out all I can about him."

Wilma sighed. Once Ada made her mind up, it was

impossible to talk her out of it. "Please don't make it awkward."

"You're creating plenty of awkwardness on your own without me having to do anything."

Wilma's mouth fell open, and then she laughed. "It's just that this is all so unexpected. I thought I'd be alone forever when Debbie and Krystal left, but now I'm feeling things I didn't think I'd feel ever again. There, I've said it."

"You're not telling me anything I don't know. We both want Obadiah to be husband number three, but we must take our time. We must make sure he is as good as he appears. If there is something off about him, I will not rest until I find out. I must choose Samuel's next best friend with caution."

Wilma blinked in surprise at Ada's words, but her friend just kept drying the dishes without skipping a beat.

CHAPTER 6

That night, Krystal and Debbie set the last of the food down the middle of the long table, then both took their seats. Wilma inhaled the aromatic aroma coming from the roast lamb. On either side of the meat were large bowls, one filled with mashed potatoes and another with macaroni and cheese.

Ada had cooked something special to accompany the lamb for dinner; her gravy was made with her secret recipe. Wilma didn't know what was in it, but it was flavorsome.

They all closed their eyes for a short prayer of gratitude before eating.

"The roast lamb smells delightful this evening," Samuel commented as Ada served him his plate with an extra helping of her signature gravy.

"Delicious, Wilma, thanks," Debbie replied.

"It's not the lamb. It's my special gravy," Ada said with a laugh.

"Oh yes, the sauce! It's extraordinary, Ada; we couldn't forget your special gravy. That's what it is!" Wilma shot Debbie a quick look, and they both attempted to contain their laughter.

Ada ignored them. Then her attention was taken with Krystal, shifting the food around her plate with her fork.

"Cheer up, Krystal. Jed might still come to Debbie's wedding. We'll make sure he knows about it," Ada said with certainty.

"Jed?" Debbie asked, confused.

"He's Malachi's brother, and we have a little something going on," Krystal responded.

"A 'little something?' You must have moved on from Matthew pretty quickly," Debbie said.

As usual, Samuel quietly ate his meal amid the conversation.

"I'm totally over Matthew. The trip away was just what I needed to forget about him."

"So, what is Jed like?" Debbie asked.

"He's amazing. He's just like me, always looking for new ways to break the rules." Krystal noticed Ada lifted her eyebrows.

Wilma broke through the awkwardness. "Krystal is joking. Jed's very masculine, isn't he, Ada? We saw him in action when one of the cows was giving birth, which had turned into a critical situation. Fortunately, Jed sorted it out and saved both mother and baby in the process."

Ada nodded. "Yes. He was brave and manly. I was

impressed, and I'm not easily impressed by anybody."

Samuel slowly nodded in agreement while cutting his meat.

"I don't understand why Matthew can't decide what he wants," Ada said, ladling more of the special gravy onto her plate. "It's shameful to have a relative who acts like that."

"It is," Krystal agreed. "But the person I feel bad for is Sigrid. She had no idea of what she was getting into. Matthew can be very persuasive and make you feel like the only girl in the world. I was a little annoyed with her at first, but she was innocent in everything when I thought about it a little more."

"I agree. There's nothing like the heartache a lost love can bring about," Wilma said.

"Then let's do something to make it up to her!" Ada suggested brightly.

"No, Ada. We must take care of our own matters. We have enough to consider with Debbie's wedding and Florence's baby arriving soon. Plus, Earl's twins are coming earlier than Florence's baby," Wilma said firmly.

"You are correct, but I still feel accountable for all of Matthew's shattered hearts. My sister is pleased thinking Samuel and I are guiding her son while Matthew has broken hearts from one end of the community to the other."

"It is not your fault," Debbie said soothingly.

"I told his mother I would watch over him while he was here, and I've failed. You do not need to make any effort, Wilma, but there must be something we can do to help Sigrid heal."

"Maybe we can find someone for her, and then she won't be upset anymore. Jed has taken my mind off him, so someone must be out there for her." Krystal suggested.

Ada nodded in agreement but wondered who would be suitable.

"I can't think of anyone." Wilma shook her head.

Suddenly, Ada sat straight in her chair with a sparkle in her eye. "I've got it!"

Debbie leaned forward, curious. "Really? Who is it?"

"Andrew Weeks. He's perfect. I always thought one of your girls would marry him, Wilma, but they had other ideas and were swept away by less obvious choices. Some were questionable, but they've all made it work."

Wilma raised her eyebrows.

Krystal considered Andrew could be perfect for Sigrid. He was stable and sensible, everything Matthew was not.

"Andrew, as in Adam's business partner?" Debbie inquired.

"*Jah*, that's the one!" Ada exclaimed. "He's perfect for Sigrid. I mean, he's not horrible to look at, and we all know he is of good character. He was raised well."

Wilma piped up, "But why hasn't he gotten married yet?"

"He has yet to find the person *Gott* meant for him!" Ada said enthusiastically.

Wilma bit her lip. Obadiah was still single. Did that mean there was something wrong with him? "Would it hurt Matthew's feelings if we proceed with this plan? He might be hoping to win back Sigrid's affections."

Krystal shook her head in response. "He's always moving on to the next woman on a whim; he'll be fine. He does a lot of flip-flopping, though, so who knows?" Her voice hinted at bitterness.

Wilma noticed Krystal's animosity toward Matthew and frowned. It wasn't healthy to hold grudges.

Ada turned to Samuel, noticing he had been silent the whole time. "Samuel, you haven't said anything yet. What's your opinion?"

Samuel smiled. "It's women's talk."

"Yes, but don't you have an opinion?" Wilma asked. "Please say if you do. You know what men think better than we do."

"As I said, it's all women's talk. Best I stay out of it." Samuel raised his hands.

"If I could sit at the big table, I could talk with Samuel. We don't like women's talk!" Jared yelled out from his small table in the corner.

"Wilma, perhaps you could invite Obadiah and Eli for dinner sometime, *jah?* Then Samuel could have some men to talk with," Ada suggested.

Wilma nodded, secretly thrilled she now had a good reason to see Obadiah again apart from their plan to show him around the town.

But it wasn't all sunshine and rainbows. In her

mind, she was concerned Ada would discover something awful about him.

She pushed that notion aside.

The warmth that flowed through her veins at the touch of Obadiah's hand was still there, and she couldn't deny she was interested in him. He was kind and sensitive. Being around him made her feel like she mattered.

It was flattering he was interested in her.

Wilma knew she couldn't just ignore her feelings forever. She couldn't let the fear of pain hold her back from happiness.

She decided to pray about it. She'd pray for clarity, guidance, and peace in her heart. If it was meant to be, she'd trust that *Gott* would make it happen in His time.

In the meantime, she'd continue to cherish their friendship and enjoy his company.

Wilma smiled as she thought about the possibility of a future with Obadiah. Maybe she'd finally found her happily ever after.

CHAPTER 7

*T*hanks to Ada's suggestion to show Obadiah around the town, Wilma nervously waited for Obadiah to arrive. All the while, she talked to herself to calm down.

We are just two friends, and we will have a few hours alone to talk in the buggy. It's not a date. We could stop somewhere for a bite to eat, but that doesn't make it a date.

She recalled it was Ada's suggestion and not his, which made this day much less like a date and more like a total embarrassment.

As Wilma stepped outside and saw Obadiah waiting with the horse and buggy, she couldn't help but feel a flutter in her stomach. She had known Obadiah for years, but something was different about this outing. Was it the way he was looking at her? Or was it the way he had dressed up for the occasion?

Obadiah helped Wilma into the buggy and took the

reins, gently urging the horse forward. They rode silently for a while, taking in the beauty of the countryside around them.

Finally, Obadiah spoke up. "I know you're hesitant, Wilma. But I promise you there's nothing to be worried about. We're just two friends out for a ride on a beautiful day."

Wilma nodded, grateful for his reassurance. But deep down, she couldn't shake the feeling there was something more to this outing.

Something bumped Wilma's shoulder, and she turned to see a large dog. "Oh." She nearly screamed.

"It's just Tiger. I didn't think you'd mind if I brought him since you love dogs."

"Oh yes." She twisted to pat Tiger on his head, and he licked her hand. "Love dogs," she said as she wiped her hand on her handkerchief.

"Sorry about that. He does like to lick."

Wilma chuckled as though she didn't mind the animal imparting its germs to her hand. "That's fine. All dogs like to lick."

As they rode along, Obadiah brought the horse to a stop at a clearing near a stream. He turned to Wilma with a smile. "How about we stop here for a picnic and fresh air?"

Wilma smiled back at him. "You brought food?"

"I did."

"I should've thought about that." This was more than just a casual outing with a friend. How he looked at her and the effort he had put into planning this day told her he had feelings for her.

They got out of the buggy, and Obadiah spread a blanket on the ground as Tiger raced from tree to tree, sniffing everything in sight.

Obadiah had packed a basket with sandwiches, fruit, and a bottle of soda. They ate and talked for hours, enjoying each other's company and the beauty of the surrounding nature.

"It's nice being out here, just the two of us. I rarely do things like this. I'm mostly at home every day," Wilma said.

"I know. You're at home looking after other people."

"I like to do that. It keeps me busy and..." her voice trailed off.

He reached out and took hold of her hand. "Who looks after you?" he asked, staring into her eyes.

She swallowed hard. "*Gott* does." It was true, and it was also the first thing that came into her head.

"You know what I mean, Wilma."

"I have friends. We look after each other."

"Perhaps you could count me among your close friends in time."

Wilma smiled at the thought, and then Ada's words rang through her head. She didn't know Obadiah or what had happened to him in the past. His firm, calloused hands still held onto hers, and she felt a warmth spread through her entire body, so she nervously withdrew her hand.

Obadiah leaned in closer to her, his eyes intense. "Wilma, I have something to confess."

Her heart skipped a beat. Was he going to say he loved her and wanted more than friendship? Or would he tell her he was married or about to be married? "Go on."

"I know we're friends, but I can't help feeling there's something more between us."

Wilma's heart was racing now. She wanted nothing more than to be with Obadiah, to feel his strong arms around her. Besides that, she loved having a man to look after. Having a man in the house made her feel safe.

"I know this might be sudden, but I must tell you how I feel about you."

She could sense where this was going, so she shook her head. She couldn't allow him to say anymore. "It's too soon."

"That's possibly true, but it's not too soon to say I feel something. I know you do too."

She bit her lip, not wanting to admit anything. She hadn't been looking for husband number three and didn't want him to think she was.

Obadiah saw the hesitation in Wilma's eyes, and he knew he had to back off. He didn't want to ruin anything, but at the same time, he couldn't ignore his feelings.

"You don't need to reply straight away, Wilma. I'm here for you, no matter what. Our friendship is important, and I don't want to lose it."

Wilma was thankful she didn't have to face an awkward conversation. She was grateful he wasn't going to rush things. "Thank you, Obadiah. Your honesty is appreciated, but I need time to think things through."

Obadiah gave her a warm, confident smile. "Take your time," he said. "I'll be returning home at some stage, but I'm unsure when. That's why I had to say something. It would be different if I lived here. We'd have all the time in the world."

Wilma made no reply, and no more was said about the matter.

The day passed in a cozy calmness as they chattered about other things and enjoyed each other's presence.

Wilma couldn't deny how her heart quickened whenever Obadiah was nearby.

"We didn't get to explore much of the town today," Obadiah remarked.

"No, but did we need to? As you said, you grew up here. Nothing has changed around these parts," Wilma replied.

Obadiah chuckled. "Not at all. I had a great time. The best time I've had in ages."

"I'm glad." Wilma looked down at Tiger, now asleep on one corner of the blanket. "Tiger seemed to have a good time too."

"He did until he wore himself out."

They stared into each other's eyes briefly before Wilma stood up. "We better get packed up. It's getting late, and I have a meal to prepare tonight. That reminds me, I'd love to have you and Eli over for a meal one night."

"I'd love that, and I'm sure Eli would too. He's always talking about how he misses Frannie's cooking and needs a decent meal."

Wilma chuckled. "He misses her a lot."

Obadiah smiled cheekily and put his hand out. Wilma put her hand out to help him, and he bounded to his feet. She noticed he hadn't offered the hand with the scar.

They packed the picnic items while Wilma wondered again how he had hurt his hand.

Once they were back at Wilma's house, Obadiah helped her out of the buggy and walked her to the front door. He turned to her, his eyes earnest. "Wilma, I know I might have caught you off guard today, but I'd like nothing more than to see where things between us could go."

Wilma knew she was starting to fall for him, but she was still guarding her heart. "Thank you for a wonderful day, Obadiah. I had a great time."

Obadiah smiled and nodded slightly. "I'm glad. We should do it again sometime."

"I'd like that." As Wilma watched him walk away, she wondered if she had given him the wrong idea by being standoffish.

What would've happened years ago if his family had never moved away? They might've married, and her life would've turned out different from what it is now.

She knew she needed to confront her fears if she

wanted to give love a chance. But the pain of losing two husbands was still fresh in her mind and in her heart.

Could she take the leap into uncertain waters?

Was she merely trying to feed an emptiness in her life? Perhaps her feelings toward him were more intense because she was so lonely.

She opened the front door, then as she closed it, she leaned against it and let out a deep sigh while ideas swirled in her head.

If she and Obadiah married, she'd become known as a woman who had married three times. She didn't even know any woman who'd been married that many times.

She'd never chosen to be a widow. Widowhood had chosen her—twice.

However, the thought of growing old alone scared her more than the fear of being labeled as a woman who'd had three husbands.

She entered the kitchen, poured herself a glass of water, and leaned against the counter. Was she meant to be alone in her older years?

There had to be a reason she never wanted to live alone. She'd always wondered if *Gott* used people's fears to teach them lessons.

If that was so, why had Obadiah come back into her life? Her biggest fear was being left alone in the house. Maybe there were no lessons to learn. What if she was blessed with a wonderful man she could grow old with?

It was a comforting thought.

She recalled the way Obadiah's eyes sparkled when

he spoke to her. The soft words he'd uttered and the way his hand had brushed against hers when he handed her a sandwich.

Now she was keen to learn anything Ada could find out about Obadiah.

CHAPTER 8

*W*ilma sat on the porch with Ada the following day, enjoying tea.

"Wilma, we should stop by Hope's house to check on Sigrid. Then we can hatch the plan we talked about."

Wilma looked up. "Plan?"

"To match Sigrid with Andrew Weeks so they can live happily and have many children. Sigrid can assimilate into our community and—"

"I remember now. I don't think I'm up for it today. I'm exhausted." Wilma replied, stifling a yawn.

Ada averted her gaze with a sigh. "I can't go alone, Wilma. Can't you tell how anxious this is making me? We should check up on her after all my nephew did to her. It's only right that we do it."

"I don't know, Ada. Is there no way you can do it yourself?"

Ada's mouth fell open at the suggestion. "Wilma, if it were you in this situation, I would be more than willing to help you, don't you think so? This is my nephew. I must right his wrongs."

Wilma put her teacup back down on its saucer and sighed. "All right, I'll go."

"*Jah,* you will," Ada replied with a smile. "Being Matthew's aunt, I feel responsible for him and his errors."

"You're not, but I understand how you feel."

Once they arrived at Hope and Fairfax's house, Wilma and Ada knocked on the front door.

Hope opened the door, and her eyebrows rose slightly as she stared from her mother to Ada and back again. "What a pleasant surprise. What are you doing here? You hardly ever visit."

"We've come to say hello," Wilma said. "We thought it was about time."

Hope stepped aside to let them in. She took their coats before leading them into the living room. They were surprised to see Bliss sitting on the couch.

"Hello, Bliss." Ada looked around. "Where's Sigrid?"

"Has she gone home?" Wilma asked.

Bliss answered, "No. She's gone for a walk. She's been gone for a while."

"I'll put the teakettle on," Hope said before heading to the kitchen.

Bliss gave a dubious frown. "Why do you want to see Sigrid? I didn't know you knew her that well."

Wilma and Ada exchanged looks before Ada said, "We thought it would be fun to set her up on a date!"

"A date? What brought about this idea?" Bliss asked.

Ada shrugged. "We are growing increasingly bored in our old age. Besides, we want everyone to be happy."

"Exactly." Wilma nodded in agreement. "That's our goal. Everyone we know must be happy."

Hope returned to the room, placing three teacups on the table—two for her guests and one for herself. Bliss was already halfway through a cup of coffee.

Hope filled each with a fragrant tea blend before she sat across from them. "This is Debbie's tea. I always buy some when I'm at the markets."

"How are you doing, Hope?" Wilma inquired.

"I'm well, thanks. Seeing you both this morning is a delightful surprise!" she replied with genuine warmth.

"They want to arrange a match for Sigrid," Bliss told Hope.

Ada noticed Bliss was acting a little strange.

"So, you two know what happened with Matthew and Sigrid then?" Hope asked.

"Yes, Krystal told us all about it," Wilma answered.

Hope looked down into her tea. "I feel awful. When I first came up with the plan about testing Matthew, I thought it was a great idea, but later I started having doubts. But, by that point, Sigrid had already arrived, and there was no turning back. The whole thing was bad for everyone concerned."

"See what happens when you meddle?" Ada asked.

The room fell silent. Wilma was waiting for

someone to tell Ada she was meddling right now, but no one dared say a word.

Eventually, Bliss spoke up, "It's alright. Everything happens for a reason. Now Krystal knows for certain Matthew isn't for her. That's all that matters, right?"

Ada and Wilma nodded in agreement.

"Bliss is here to talk about Adam's birthday. The four of us usually—"

"The four of you? You mean you normally celebrate Adam's birthday without us?" Wilma stared at Bliss.

"That's right. Adam doesn't make a fuss about his birthday. We normally have a special meal with Hope and Fairfax."

"Well, Adam will have a special birthday dinner at Wilma's house this time. Oh, and be sure to invite Andrew Weeks." Ada grinned.

"Why do you want Andrew to come?" Bliss asked.

Now it was Wilma's turn to have some input. "That's right. Adam and Andrew work together, *jah?*"

"That's right." Bliss nodded.

"Well, they must be great friends." Wilma grinned.

"They are."

"So, it makes sense to invite him too for his friend's birthday," Ada said.

"I'm not sure what Adam will think—"

Wilma interrupted Bliss. "Make sure Sigrid comes to the birthday dinner."

"I see what you're doing," Bliss said.

Ada clapped her hands. "That's settled then. Let's do that on Friday night next week. If you already have plans, cancel them. Don't allow Sigrid to leave town until after the dinner." Ada turned to Wilma.

"Why so far off?" Wilma asked.

"That will give us plenty of time to organize things."

"Do either of you care that Bliss just said Adam never wants a fuss made over his birthday?" Hope asked.

"Everyone says that. They don't mean it." Ada grinned.

Wilma sighed, knowing they'd have to let them in on what they were doing. "We have a plan, and it's not about Adam. It's about Sigrid. We thought Andrew Weeks and Sigrid would make a good pair. There's no harm in it. How can there be any harm in love?"

Suddenly, Ada grabbed Wilma's arm, making her jump. "Oh my, Wilma, it's Tuesday."

Wilma frowned at Ada. "Yes?"

"Daphne and Susan are coming to your place for our little get-together."

Wilma bounded to her feet. "Oh no. With our recent change of routine, I nearly forgot. What's the time?"

"It's late." Ada stood. "I'm sorry, Hope, but we'll be back in touch. Make sure Sigrid is at the birthday dinner for Adam on Friday night and invite anyone else you think should be there."

"But not Matthew," Wilma called over her shoulder on the way to the door.

Hope got up to show them out. "We'll make sure Andrew Weeks comes too. Sigrid does need something good to happen to her after her disappointment."

Ada smiled. "But that's not enough. Someone needs to give them both a little push so they can see the possibilities."

Wilma tapped Ada on her shoulder. "Let's go, Ada."

Both of them hurried out the door.

CHAPTER 9

*A*da and Wilma had managed to arrive home before their guests got there. Wilma hastily cut up some fruit and then she found a packet of marshmallows in the back of the pantry.

There were no cookies from Ada that morning, but Susan and Daphne arrived bringing food with them. Susan had baked raspberry and white chocolate muffins, and Daphne had made rocky road chocolate.

Wilma's eyes lit up at the sight of all the delicious food on the small table in the middle of the living room.

"So, how was your trip?" Daphne mumbled around a mouthful of rocky road.

"It was great. Cherish loved the quilt." Wilma sipped her tea.

"It was a lovely quilt after you added the appliqué, Wilma. Very unusual," Daphne said fondly.

"Just like Cherish," Ada commented. "The unusual part."

"Oh, Ada," Wilma said with a chuckle, making everyone laugh.

"I'm only joking. She is growing up into a lovely young lady."

"We met Malachi's brother, Jed, while we were there, didn't we, Ada?" Wilma expected Ada to chime in and then carry the conversation along. She always enjoyed sharing the latest gossip. But this time, Ada simply nodded and blew on her hot tea.

Wilma thought it was strange for Ada not to say anything about Jed since he was a unique character. "Krystal and Jed hit it off very well. He's fascinated with her, and she appears to be just as caught up with him."

Daphne gasped as a hand flew up to cover her mouth. "I'm overjoyed for her! This is fantastic news."

"Especially after all the grief Matthew caused her. Oops, sorry, Ada. That was uncalled for," Susan said apologetically, shaking her head.

"It's alright, Susan." Ada attempted to mask her irritation over Susan's continual apologies with a roll of her eyes.

Wilma noticed the interaction and gave Susan a comforting pat on the shoulder to defuse the tension caused by Ada's reaction.

"Is something the matter, Ada? You are a little quieter than normal." Daphne tilted her head curiously.

"Now you mention it, I have had something on my

mind. I was thinking about what happened at the bishop's house when we were there. Oh, you would not believe it if I told you." Ada looked upward, shaking her head.

Wilma gulped as heat rushed to her cheeks. She thought this might become a topic of conversation, although she wished it hadn't come up.

"What happened?" Daphne asked Ada.

Ada looked over at Wilma. "Shall I tell them?"

Wilma shrugged and gave a nod. Now that Ada had opened her mouth, she knew the ladies wouldn't let up until they knew what had happened.

Ada smiled, blinked a couple of times, and then began. "We went to the bishop's place for information about the daughter Christina adopted out."

Susan gasped. "When was this?"

"Ages ago before she married Mark."

"I had no idea," Susan said.

"I knew. It was a child she had out of wedlock." Daphne gave a nod. "Do go on, Ada."

"We had planned to observe the children without asking any questions. We were going to talk about the weather or other things that didn't matter. However, Wilma couldn't keep her mouth shut. As soon as the bishop's poor wife opened the door, Wilma declared we knew all her children were adopted and requested she reveal which one was Christina's daughter. And, what's worse was we didn't even know for certain if one of the bishop's children is Christina's daughter."

Daphne and Susan exchanged shocked glances and

then turned to Wilma. "Is what Ada said true?" Daphne asked.

"Unfortunately, yes, but I wasn't in control of my actions, was I, Ada?"

Ada shook her head. "No. Wilma took too many illicit substances and, on top of that, had way too much strong coffee."

Susan gasped and covered her mouth while Daphne's eyes widened like saucers. "Did you do that, Wilma?"

Wilma frowned. "Oh, Ada. How much worse are you trying to make this? Since when are headache tablets illicit substances?" Wilma turned to both Susan and Daphne, who seemed terribly concerned. "All I took were headache tablets, and Ada had me drink way too much coffee on top. The coffee and the tablets did not mix."

"I didn't mean anything bad, Wilma. Headache tablets are technically dr—"

"Don't say *that* word." Wilma held up her hand.

Daphne stifled a chuckle as she pushed her glasses further up on her nose. "I've never heard of headache pills making someone act that way before."

Ada gave a hearty sigh. "It was tough to witness."

"Did you manage to find any information on Christina's daughter in the end?" Daphne asked.

"No!" Ada said. "The bishop's wife kicked us out and told us never to return. She was so mad that her face was as red as their barn. And I can tell you their barn was very red."

"It was terrible," Wilma murmured, recalling the scene.

"We were all scared that Cherish was about to get into some kind of trouble with the bishop," Ada added.

"Of course," Daphne said. "That's understandable."

"But Malachi is the bishop's nephew, which has to help." Looking back, Ada could see the funny side, but it certainly was not funny at the time. "Then things got worse." Ada figured she'd told them that much; she had to tell them the rest.

"There's more?" Susan asked in disbelief.

Wilma felt awful listening to Ada repeat the biggest error of her life.

"*Jah*. Listen up. When we returned to Cherish's farm, Leonie, the bishop's wife, came to the house. She had calmed down. After we talked for a while, she let us off the hook, but her warning was clear. If we ever messed with her family again, there would be consequences." Ada shook her head, making tsk tsk sounds with her tongue.

"Oh, dear. How awful to be in a position like that," Daphne said.

Wilma shifted in her seat, hoping to change the conversation. "So it seems like we won't find out who Christina's daughter is anytime soon. I guess we'll wait until she's eighteen or some such thing. I hope and pray she'll come looking for her mother."

"I'm sorry, Wilma, I think you mean her birthmother," Susan corrected her.

"Yes, that's what I meant."

"Not a word to Christina, though. She knows none of this." Ada put her finger up to her lips.

The atmosphere in the room shifted with an uncomfortable stillness. Wilma nervously tapped her fingers on her teacup as Ada glanced around, perplexed by the sudden quietness. She turned to Susan, who now looked like a scared rabbit. "Why do you keep staring at Wilma?" Ada questioned her.

"I'm just surprised by what you did, Wilma. Going to her house like that and saying what you said. I didn't think you would do something like that, I'm sorry to say."

Wilma groaned and looked down at her hands. "I know. It wasn't my best moment, that's for sure. I can't blame the illicit... I mean the tablets. I must take full responsibility for my actions."

"In lighter news," Ada said, shifting in her chair. "An old friend has come back to town from our childhood!"

"Who is it?" Susan asked, her round face beaming.

"Obadiah."

"Obadiah?" Daphne frowned.

"That's right." Wilma nodded nervously, hoping Ada wouldn't tell them her secret about being in love with him from an early age. Reliving the interaction with the bishop's wife was all the embarrassment she could handle for one day.

"Ahh, how lovely. I hope to bump into him. Let me see. His folks moved to a community up north when Obadiah would have been still in his teens," Daphne said.

"I wouldn't know him. I'm sorry," Susan said. "I wasn't living here back then."

Ada huffed and turned to Susan. "You don't need to keep saying you're sorry. If I had a dime for every time you said it, I'd be able to purchase a brand new buggy with a heater and possibly a horse too."

Susan bit her lip, and everyone looked at her, waiting for her to say she was sorry for saying sorry, but she didn't.

Wilma felt sorry for Susan. "That's right, Susan, you wouldn't know Obadiah."

Daphne tapped her chin. "Let me see now. Obadiah has older brothers and one sister, if I remember correctly."

"You know everything, Daphne," Ada said.

"I make it my business to find out almost everything, seeing I keep all the genealogy records for our community."

"I just want to say one thing," Susan said. Everyone looked over at her. Susan seldom had much to say. "I won't say it again."

Ada scoffed. "You might need to say it at some stage if the circumstances call for it. I don't mean for you never to say it again. Just don't say it in every sentence."

Susan nodded and looked down at her hands in her lap.

Wilma leaned forward and picked up the teapot. "More tea, anyone?"

CHAPTER 10

Since Malachi and Simon had already left to work on Favor and Simon's house, Wally and Caramel followed Cherish. "Have you thought about what you're going to do today?" Cherish asked while taking an early morning stroll with Favor.

"Hmm." Favor inhaled the crisp morning air as she gazed at the rising sun. "My house is coming along beautifully. I'll most likely spend the day there. I can start planning where I'll put everything."

"Everything? You didn't bring much with you."

"I don't care. We'll get everything eventually. We've got swags we can sleep on until we can get a bed."

"Nonsense. Take some furniture from here. You can take one of the beds from the spare rooms and any other furniture you want. There's plenty of stuff."

"Thanks. We might take you up on that offer. I'll talk to Simon about it."

"Sure. I can't think why he'd have a problem with it."

"What do you have planned for today? Do you want to come with me, or do you have stuff to do here?" Favor asked.

"I've got a few things I need to purchase from in town. Then I'll be over this afternoon. I'll drive you there, and I'll continue to the store."

"Okay, sounds perfect!"

"I've been wondering how you're adapting to your new life. I'm sure it's not the same as being in your own house with Simon, but how are you feeling about making this move so far?"

Favor grinned. "It's incredible, Cherish. I feel so liberated. We can make our own choices now and plan a family on our terms."

"It took a while for me to believe you'd ever be released from Harriet's hold. I never thought she'd let Simon go."

"Shh. Cherish, we shouldn't talk like that anymore. I'm trying to turn over a new leaf."

"New life, new leaf?" Cherish said with a soft chuckle.

"Exactly! When I was there last, Harriet showed me an aspect of her personality I'd never seen before. I shouldn't have been mean about her before."

"So, she's changed? What aspect of her personality did you see?"

"A good one. Hopefully, distance will strengthen the

heart, and it won't be so hard when they finally move here."

"Do you think it will happen anytime soon?"

"It's still a while off. They said it'll take a long time to sell their farm. We made our intentions clear; they know they need to give us time to get settled in. I don't think they'll sell the farm, though. They say they will, but they'll have a hard time letting go."

"Hmm. I'm sensing a pattern," Cherish said.

"The more I think about it, the more I think they might not make the move."

"We'll just have to wait and see," Cherish said as she tossed a ball across the farm. Caramel took off at lightning speed after the ball, with Wally waddling behind him, honking furiously.

Later that day, Cherish strolled through the store, relishing having the ability to buy whatever she wanted without worrying about the price tag.

Before she knew they were rich, she was so careful about money, counting out every cent and making do with everything they already had, no matter how worn out it was. Today, that was all going to change. She filled her shopping cart with new kitchenware, plush pillows, soft towels, luxurious sheets, fancy cushions, and placemats until the shopping cart overflowed.

Cherish realized she needed to slow down before the cart got too heavy to push. As she wheeled it around the corner, she spotted an enormous sofa that would fit perfectly in Simon and Favor's home.

She wanted to do something kind for them to make

their home feel more comfortable. After all, they had traveled so far with nothing but suitcases of clothes. The price tag made her eyes widen. She'd never bought a couch before.

Were they always so pricey?

She was still using Aunt Dagmar's furniture that had come with the house.

The couch would make an excellent gift for Favor.

Sam, who owned the store, strolled over. "Like the couch, eh?"

"I do. I've never seen furniture here."

"Someone ordered it from the catalog but didn't like it when it came in."

"Oh." Cherish's mind ticked over. It was meant to be. "I'll take it."

Sam stepped back, clearly shocked. "You will?"

"Yes."

He smiled and rubbed his hands together. "I'll bring it to you tomorrow, Cherish, free of charge."

"No. It's not for me. I'm buying it for my sister and her husband. They've just moved here. I'll introduce you next time she's in the store."

"Okay. When you've finished shopping, give me the address and we can arrange a time."

"Thank you."

After taking care of the payment and scheduling for the furniture to be delivered to Simon and Favor's home later, Cherish loaded up the back of the buggy with her items and returned home to unpack them.

It took Cherish five trips back and forth from the

house to the buggy to get everything inside. Everywhere she looked, there were bags with items spilling out of them.

She found a catalog tucked away in one of the shopping bags and began flipping through it. On the first page, she saw a selection of wooden beds, handcrafted and beautiful. It was obvious there was excellent craftsmanship in each item.

They would look great in her home and probably Simon and Favor's too. She decided she would order new beds for all of them.

After all, what else was Malachi going to do with his money? *No, our money,* Cherish thought.

As Cherish finished with the catalog and began unloading the bags, Malachi walked through the door. He took off his hat and froze when he saw the results of her shopping spree.

He didn't look happy, and that made Cherish feel awful.

The new things had made her happy. "What are you doing here? After unpacking, I was about to meet you at Simon and Favor's."

"I had completely forgotten to give Wally his kibble today, so I thought I'd come back and have lunch with you and do that. So, what's going on in here?" He placed his hands on his hips as he looked around. "Are we opening a store that I didn't know about?"

She shrugged her shoulders and tried to downplay the situation. "I needed to pick up a few things we need."

"More than a few, it looks like!"

"And I got Simon and Favor an amazing couch for their housewarming gift."

Malachi gasped in surprise. "A new couch? That must have been pricey."

"I'm also getting a new couch from the catalog tomorrow, and we need a new bed. Not just for us either - every bed in the house needs to be updated. We haven't bought anything new since we've been married. This is all Aunt Dagmar's stuff. Don't you think we should have things that are ours?"

"No! That's not necessary. We already have everything we need here. We don't need any of this extra stuff. There's plenty of use left in everything we already have. I thought you liked using Aunt Dagmar's things."

"Malachi, please, stop worrying so much," Cherish said softly as she stood before him, gently placing her hands on his shoulders. "We are surrounded by old stuff. I thought we could have new things. After all, we don't need to worry about money because we're rich."

Malachi shook his head. "Not for much longer if you keep doing things like this."

Cherish felt the sting of his words and pulled away from him. She knew he was only looking out for their finances, but it felt like he was taking away her independence.

"I can't even buy some new things for the house without you making me feel guilty," she said, tears welling in her eyes.

"I'm not trying to make you feel guilty, Cherish. I

want us to be responsible with our money. We can discuss what to do with it, but I prefer you avoid going off and spending money alone. There are people out there who need money and—"

"I know, but sometimes it feels like you don't trust me to make decisions."

"That's not true. I trust you, but we need to be cautious with our spending. We don't want to end up like those lottery winners who go broke in a few years because they don't know how to manage their finances."

Cherish wiped her tears and took a deep breath. She knew he was right, but she also wanted to enjoy their newfound wealth and surround herself with pretty things. "We're living on my farm. I never bring that up because I consider it our farm."

"Okay, I understand. I'm sorry if I came across as harsh, but I'm shocked at all this stuff. We don't need it."

Cherish looked around. There was a lot of stuff. "I could try taking it back."

He smiled. "There's no need to do that. The way I was raised, we never let anything go to waste. We never got anything new until the item was broken beyond repair or completely worn out."

"I'll be more mindful of our spending," she said, trying to compose herself. "But can we at least get a new bed and maybe a couch? It would make our home feel more like ours."

He looked down. "I don't know."

She looked over at Timmy and Tommy in their cage. "Perhaps I'm getting the nesting instinct, and I'm building a nest ready to raise our family. Birds always bring in new twigs and things to prepare their nest."

Malachi frowned at her.

She knew her argument was weak. "We can afford it, Malachi. I don't think I'm asking a lot. I just like to be surrounded by nice things and have some comfort. You know that couch isn't comfortable and the mattress we have is a bit lumpy."

Malachi sighed, then nodded. "We can meet halfway. You're right. We don't need to be so frugal all the time. We can get some new things every now and again. But let's do some research first before we buy large items and find things within a reasonable budget. We don't need to have a top-of-the-range bed or couch."

Cherish smiled, feeling relieved that they could compromise. "Thank you, Malachi. I promise we'll be responsible with our money."

Malachi pulled her into a hug. "I know we will. We're in this together, remember?"

Cherish nodded, feeling grateful for her husband's practicality and support. As they embraced, she couldn't help but feel content. They were rich, but they still had each other, which was worth more than any material possessions in the world.

CHAPTER 11

*B*y the end of the Sunday meeting at Willersburg, everyone congregated out in the back of the new meeting house. They chatted while they feasted on a sumptuous spread, but Jed stood isolated from the rest, yearning for Krystal. In his mind, he envisioned them as a couple and wondered how he could take care of her.

Suddenly, he thought that if Malachi were to loan him some money, he could purchase one of the plots of land and build them a house. That way, Krystal would end up living close to Favor, her best friend. It seemed perfect.

He surveyed the long table in front of him that was filled with delectable dishes. The sizzling aroma of pork lifted to his nostrils, and he grabbed some before admiring the mashed potatoes, salad, homemade bread and butter, roasted vegetables, chicken drumsticks, and macaroni cheese; the selection was never-ending. The meal held after the meetings weren't normally this good. Today they were celebrating the opening of the new meeting house, which also doubled as the community's school. It was an idea thought up by the bishop to make the meetings more accessible for everyone.

Suddenly the bishop arrived at his side and began filling his plate with food. "Jed, it's nice to see you."

"Nice to see you again, Uncle Zachariah," he commented before picking up a piece of chicken in his fingers and popping it into his mouth.

"How have you been?" the bishop asked.

"I'm doing well. I've got plans to visit Lancaster County soon." Jed was a little surprised at the words that tumbled out of his mouth. He knew he had to see Krystal, but he wasn't sure when he'd actually do it.

"Oh really? Any special reason?" the bishop asked.

"A very special reason. I met someone recently."

"Is this one of Cherish's companions?"

"Yes."

"I'm glad to hear it. Are you planning a prolonged visit?"

"Well, I'm not sure. It'll depend on how things pan out when I get there. Maybe I can talk her into returning with me. That's the plan so far." Jed chuckled. There was something about his uncle that always pulled information out of him.

The bishop nodded. "I hope things will go well. Enjoy your trip," he said before he stepped away and started walking back toward his table.

"Wait! Uncle, I have a question."

He stopped and turned back around to face him. "Yes?"

"Are there still any plots of cheap land available for sale?"

"There's one block left. Why, are you interested?"

"Just curious."

"You know it's only for couples, right?"

"Hmm. Is that what the seller said?" Jed still hadn't revealed to his uncle that he knew Malachi owned the land.

The bishop nodded.

"I'll see what I can do to make this woman my wife, and then, who knows?"

The bishop nodded. "Let me know."

"You'll be one of the first." Jed grabbed a second bread roll before heading over and plonking himself down beside Malachi, who was seated next to Cherish.

He gave Favor and Cherish a warm smile. He felt like he had sisters. He couldn't quite understand why Cherish was with Malachi, but she seemed happy with him. Malachi was talking to him now, and he felt more and more comfortable the longer he stayed there. He knew he had changed within himself. He had become a better person. Could Malachi see that? As everyone else around them began to chatter between themselves, Jed leaned in closer to Malachi and said, "I have something to ask you before I go."

"What is it?"

"Uncle Zachariah just mentioned a block of land is

still available. Can you put it aside for me so I can pay for it later?"

Malachi was surprised Jed knew about it. "You'll have to ask the bishop about that. It's not something I'm aware of."

Jed let out a noisy breath before fixing his gaze on his brother. "I already looked up the deed, Malachi. And I know you own it, and you owned all the land before it was sold."

Malachi paused for a few seconds before responding, "I'll have to consider it. It's meant to be reserved for married couples."

"If things go as I hope they will, I plan on being a married man in the near future."

Malachi was aware that if Krystal and Jed got together, Cherish would be ecstatic if Krystal moved here, and so would Favor.

"Like I said, I'll think about it. Don't let anyone else know I own the land."

"Thank you, brother. Your secret is safe with me."

CHAPTER 12

rystal unsuccessfully fought the urge to daydream in the middle of the sermon at the Sunday meeting. She sat next to Debbie and Wilma and pondered her future.

Would Jed come to live in Lancaster County if things worked out between them?

Leaving behind the quilt store filled with so many memories was almost impossible for her to imagine. She couldn't leave. Jed had no job. It would be so much easier if he moved to her community.

She dreamed of the day she would see him again. Jed was unlike the other men Krystal had met in the community. While she felt like everyone else judged her for not being born Amish, Jed never regarded that as an issue.

It may have been odd to others that he drove a car while they traveled by horse and buggy, but to Krystal, this was ordinary; after all, it was how she had grown up. It wasn't a big deal to her. Yes, he was a rule-breaker, but he hurt no one by driving a car.

She had never felt so accepted, understood, and appreciated by a man.

The real question was, was Jed feeling the same way about her? Was he thinking about her every moment of the day? He had hinted at his feelings, but she didn't know if that was because she was there and if out of sight was… out of mind.

Krystal headed toward the place where dinner was being served. She hadn't taken in anything that had been discussed - her thoughts were occupied by Jed alone.

As Krystal mingled with the other guests, she saw Sigrid up ahead. She was still here, and Krystal felt annoyed at the sight of the woman who'd turned Matthew's head.

When everyone began to disperse toward the food table, Krystal noticed Wilma and Ada already seated with Debbie and Jared, so she joined them.

"Why the long face, Krystal?" Wilma queried as Krystal took a seat.

"Thinking about Jed?" Ada interjected with her usual smirk when she thought she was being amusing.

"Yeah. I'm just wondering when I'll see him again," she answered truthfully. There was no point denying her feelings. They saw how she'd been around him back at Cherish's farm.

"It'll happen when and if God wills it." Debbie smiled as she buttered a piece of bread.

"Have you had the chance to catch up with Sigrid yet?" Ada inquired, abruptly switching topics.

"I haven't talked to her if that's what you're asking."

Suddenly a figure approached their table, and Krystal looked up to meet Matthew's gaze. As soon as he saw Krystal, he stopped dead in his tracks, waved hesitatingly, then took tentative steps in different directions before turning and walking away. It was so awkward. Everyone saw what he did, but no one commented.

"I've been thinking about how to get Sigrid and Andrew together," Ada said between munching on a chicken drumstick.

"Why don't we just invite them for dinner?" Krystal proposed.

"We have that all taken care of. We're having a birthday evening for Adam, and we told Bliss to make sure they bring along Andrew," Ada replied with her mouth full.

Wilma nodded in agreement. "And Hope is bringing Sigrid."

"I don't think that's the greatest idea now I think about it some more. What if she gets twice as hurt somehow," Krystal said.

Ada rolled her eyes. "We have to make amends for what Matthew did wrong."

"Wow. That'll keep you busy if that's what you're doing." Krystal pressed her lips together and noticed Ada didn't look pleased with her comment.

"I believe they will be a great couple. I hate to point

this out, Krystal, but maybe you should look at your part in how Sigrid got hurt," Ada pointed out.

Krystal cast her gaze downwards. Ada was right. She had tested Matthew, and it had led to Sigrid being hurt.

"I see now I acted selfishly," Krystal said, looking at her hands. "I didn't think about the consequences of my actions or how they could hurt others."

Debbie placed a reassuring hand on Krystal's shoulder and smiled at her kindly.

"Don't be hard on yourself. We all make mistakes, even Ada." Wilma grinned.

Ada's eyes opened wide. "I make very few mistakes. I can't even think of the last one I made, Wilma."

Just then, everyone fell silent as Obadiah approached them. "Good afternoon. I am Obadiah. We haven't met yet." Obadiah smiled at Krystal and Debbie and offered his hand to Krystal, who shook it in response. Krystal vaguely recalled the bishop introducing the man before the meeting had started. She would have remembered his name had Jed not occupied her thoughts. Wilma glanced up from her food with a faint smile on her face.

"Lovely to meet you. I'm Krystal."

"And I'm Debbie," Debbie said as she stood to shake his hand.

Obadiah smiled as he looked at Wilma. "It is wonderful to encounter you again, Wilma. May I join you?"

Wilma liked the way he spoke so correctly. She

grabbed her napkin and wiped her lips before responding. "Please, be my guest."

Krystal watched with delight as she saw Wilma fixated on Obadiah. She had never seen Wilma view someone that way before; it was clear as day she found him attractive. She wondered if anyone else had picked up on their obvious connection. She glanced over at Debbie and saw her smiling at the couple.

Wilma noticed them all staring at her. "Obadiah is an old friend. He used to live here many years ago."

"Oh, how amazing." Krystal smiled.

"Krystal and Debbie live with me at the Orchard."

"Are they your daughters?" Obadiah asked.

Wilma chuckled. "No, but in a way, they are like daughters to me. Debbie was Levi's niece, and Krystal is—"

Krystal interrupted. "A stranger from another land. I was born an *Englisher,* and I joined when I came to stay with Wilma's family."

Ada nodded. "A week with Wilma's family turned into a lifetime."

"A true delight to meet you both." Obadiah beamed at them, and Krystal felt a warmth radiating from him that made her instantly take a liking.

"Hey! What about me?" Jared interjected, causing laughter to break out around the table.

"We could never forget you, Jared!" Debbie said as she ruffled his hair.

"This is my little friend, Jared. He's Debbie's son," Wilma said.

Ada looked at Jared disapprovingly. Debbie knew she thought Jared was too vocal and should have sat quietly without saying a word. But Debbie was pleased Jared was becoming more social and wasn't shy around people.

Krystal and Debbie looked at Wilma and the man sitting opposite them; both had stars in their eyes. The pair continued to gaze lovingly at each other until, finally, Wilma looked away, taking a bite out of her roll.

Krystal couldn't help but chuckle when she noticed how agitated Wilma appeared. It was clear she was strongly attracted to him.

"It's been ages since you two have seen each other, right?" Debbie asked.

"That's right. Even after my family moved away when I was young, I never forgot about this town - or Wilma." Obadiah paused and smiled at Wilma, who, in turn, blushed.

"That's sweet. Anyway, Debbie, I'm starving! Would you like to come and get food with me?" Krystal asked.

Debbie looked up from her food, momentarily confused, until she realized what Krystal was doing. "Yes. I'll come. Jared, you can come with us too."

"Aww. Do I have to? I want to stay with Aunt Wilma."

"Yes, you have to. There might be some nice desserts."

Jared leaped off his seat and grabbed his mother's hand, and the three of them left Wilma alone with Obadiah.

"Desserts?" Ada asked. "In that case, I'll come too." Ada hurried to catch up with them.

Their absence made Wilma feel like she could breathe.

"How are you today, Wilma?" he asked.

"I'm fine. How are you enjoying your stay so far?"

"I love it. I enjoy catching up with you and learning about your life."

Wilma couldn't help but smile. "A lot has happened for both of us. The other day, I thought about how we used to swim in the lake together."

Obadiah's eyes widened as he covered his mouth. "I'm sorry for my bad behavior."

Wilma nodded. "You remember?"

Obadiah bit his lip. "I do."

"You used to run after me, splash me, and then push me in when I wasn't paying attention."

"It's true. I gave you a hard time. I'm sorry for that. It could've been dangerous."

Wilma chuckled. "I survived. We did some dangerous things as children, but things were different back then."

"I only pushed you in because I had strong feelings for you and didn't know how to express it."

Wilma felt her insides twist as Obadiah spoke. It had been many years since she'd experienced this kind of nervousness; it was how she used to feel around Josiah, her first husband. Her throat was tight, and she found herself unable to speak. Fortunately, Ada returned with a bowl of chopped fruit laced with custard and sat across from them.

"Obadiah, Wilma and I are hosting a dinner this Thursday, and we would like you to join us if you can."

"I would be delighted to attend. Thank you."

"And bring Eli with you, of course."

"I will. I can answer for him right now. We'll both be there."

Wilma faced her own shame for not having given him a time when she mentioned having them for dinner the last time she saw him.

CHAPTER 13

On Monday, Debbie parked her buggy in the shade outside Jared's school and went inside. She quickly located him sketching alone in a corner and walked over to him. When he noticed her, he leaped up from his seat and embraced her tightly. "Mommy, I've missed you so much!"

Debbie gave a little laugh and messed up his hair. "I've missed you too, son. How was school?"

Jared released an enthusiastic shout as he bounced on the spot. "It was great!"

"I'm glad to hear. Let's go say goodbye to Miss Dibble." Debbie took Jared's hand and guided him toward the teacher, who was sitting behind a large desk.

"Ah, Debbie. It's good to have you here." Miss Dibble took off her glasses and placed them on the desk.

"Nice to see you. Thank you for today."

"It's my pleasure. I'm impressed by Jared's reading skills."

Debbie looked down at Jared, who was beaming with joy.

"Where did you learn to read, Jared?" Miss. Dibble asked.

Jared didn't answer. He was swatting at a flying insect. Debbie had to answer for him. "My Uncle Levi taught him to read from the newspaper."

"He must have taken in a lot of it because he's an advanced reader. He's at a level three years above his age."

"Incredible!" Debbie was astonished. "Fantastic job, Jared. I'm so pleased with you!"

The insect had gone, and Jared was able to focus. He looked up at his mother. "I do a very good job in school, *Mamm*."

"I believe it!"

The teacher chuckled heartily before saying, "Behave for your mother, and I'll see you tomorrow, Jared."

"Okay, Bye!" Jared turned around and ran for the door. Debbie waved goodbye to the teacher as she hurried after him to stop him from running onto the road.

When they arrived back at the orchard, Jared colored at his table in the kitchen while Debbie sat at the table drinking tea with Ada and Wilma.

"Jared's doing so well in school. The teacher said he's reading years above his level."

Ada raised her eyebrows. "Wow. That's surprising," she said, trying not to sound too shocked.

"Jared, is it true?" Wilma asked.

Jared looked up from his table and nodded. "Yep! *Onkel* Levi taught me how to be super smart!"

Wilma felt herself getting choked up. Debbie noticed and placed a hand on her shoulder.

"You're a good boy."

"*Denke,* Aunt Wilma. And you're a good aunt."

Wilma chuckled, and even Ada smiled at his remark.

"Oh, there's a letter for you, Debbie," Wilma said, pointing at the counter.

Debbie jumped up and rushed over, hoping it was from Fritz. Her heart skipped a beat as she picked up the envelope with Fritz's writing. She read the letter in the living room before returning to sit at the kitchen bench with the ladies.

"Fritz?" Ada asked.

"Yes."

"How is he?" Wilma asked.

"He's good. He says he's missing me."

Ada could sense something was off in the way Debbie spoke. "What's wrong?"

"It's nothing," Debbie shook her head as she folded the letter and placed it inside her apron pocket.

"You know we are a lot older and experienced with this type of thing," Wilma said.

"We give excellent advice, too," Ada said, nodding.

"It's nothing. It's just that no date has been set yet. I

know we will be married at the end of the year, but when? Why has no date been set? It's hard to arrange a wedding with no wedding date."

"Have you asked Fritz to confirm a date?"

"I didn't want to appear too clingy and desperate by bothering him with questions. Will he be back in time for the wedding? Certainly, he'd need to move here before that event. There is so much uncertainty, and nothing seems clear."

"I'm certain you have nothing to worry about. Fritz is a good man, and he's doing the right thing, wrapping up the loose ends at home so he can dedicate himself to you when he moves here," Wilma spoke while reaching for a cookie.

"Let's hope that's true," Debbie said as her gaze flicked over to Jared, smiling a little as his soft humming filled the room.

"Is there anything else on your mind?" Ada inquired.

"I'm not sure about the wedding dresses. Florence is significantly pregnant, and once the baby is born, she'll be too busy to make them."

"We told you we can help with that—Ada and I will sew them for you. We said we would already."

"And, like always, we'll take care of all the food, so you don't have to worry about that either," Ada smiled warmly.

"Thank you, that's very helpful."

"Have you chosen your attendants yet?"

Debbie took a moment to consider. "I still haven't decided. I have so many friends. I'm close to Florence, but she'll be busy with the baby by then. There's Krystal, I'll have to have her as an attendant, and I'm also close with Bliss and Hope."

"Hmm, you didn't mention Joy," Ada observed, raising an eyebrow.

Debbie breathed out heavily. "We're not close like we once were. I mean, she no longer looks after Jared. Not that she needs to anymore because he's in school."

"She could look after him after school like Bliss does sometimes."

Wilma frowned at Ada's comment. Everyone knew Joy and Debbie had a minor tiff over Jared and his behavior. No one needed to say it out aloud. "You need to start making some decisions soon. Before moving forward, we need to decide the number of dresses and kind of cakes for the event," Wilma said to divert the conversation.

"Okay. I know you're right."

"What about pies? Cherry and apple sound nice," Ada suggested.

Wilma piped up, "I love caramel and raspberry tarts."

Ada turned up her nose. "Caramel and raspberry together, or do you mean separately?"

Wilma shook her head. "No, of course not! Individual ones - one type with caramel and another one with raspberry."

Ada rolled her eyes while Debbie chuckled at their chatter. She wasn't concerned with the food. She knew Ada and Wilma would do an excellent job.

CHAPTER 14

That evening when Krystal got home, she took her place on the porch and read a book in the fading light of day. Taking a moment to look upward, she savored the spectacular sunset with its breathtaking array of orange and pink. Crickets chirped around her, and she hoped they'd stay in the bushes and not come close.

She pulled her shawl across her shoulders against the chill of the air as she went back to reading the novel someone had accidentally left in her store. When she heard a sound, she saw Matthew approaching the house.

"What does he want?" she grumbled to herself.

Matthew stepped up on the porch, stood before her, and inquired, "Krystal, may I sit with you?"

Somewhat begrudgingly, Krystal replied, "Okay." She closed her book and put it on her lap as he sat across from her.

"How are you?" he queried.

"I'm doing well.

"What are you reading?" Matthew gestured to the book in her lap.

Krystal looked at the novel and was embarrassed that the couple on the cover stared into each other's eyes. It was clearly a romance novel. "Someone left it in my store. I was checking to see if there was a name or a phone number in it to locate the owner."

"Don't bother. It's just a book. It's not valuable or anything."

Krystal shifted nervously in her seat, slightly uncomfortable about why Matthew was there. "What brings you by tonight?"

"I came here to see you."

"For what reason? You don't have to apologize again. I've already let it go. I've moved on in more ways than one."

"You have?"

Krystal nodded. "I have."

"So then... do you believe…"

Krystal's eyebrows arched as she wondered what he was trying to say. Was he really attempting to reconcile again? She couldn't take his double-mindedness any longer.

Before he could utter another word, she knew she had to put an end to it. Her heart was already taken by Jed. She was sure about him now; Jed was the one for her.

"I've met someone else," she said firmly.

Matthew leaned back in the chair. "No."

"Yes, I have"

"Who is it?"

"Just someone. Someone you don't know," she replied. "I'm sorry things didn't work out for us, but it was never meant to be."

"I haven't seen you with anyone in our community. Is this real, or are you trying to make me jealous? If you're doing that, you don't need to."

Krystal shrugged, leaving Matthew slightly annoyed at her lack of response.

Krystal's silence was designed to stop her from saying what she really thought of his comment.

"It's getting chilly, and dinner will be ready soon. I should get inside." She rose from the chair and began walking toward the door.

"Hold on. This can't be the end. I care about you," Matthew pleaded.

Krystal wasn't surprised. It was the same old Matthew and the same old back and forth. It angered her that he wasn't listening to her, and he kept trying to persuade her. "I'm sorry, Matthew. But you blew your chance long ago," Krystal said firmly.

"I understand how I let you down. Sigrid wasn't for me, so I left her. I haven't been able to stop thinking about you. Can you please give me another opportunity? I'll do whatever it takes." Matthew got down and kneeled in front of her with his hands clasped together, pleading.

Now the only feeling she had for him was pity. "I

told you I've moved on. There's someone new in my life now," she said softly.

"Okay, I'll let it be if you tell me who the new man is." He looked up at her refusing to get up.

Krystal shook her head and turned away, not bothering to answer. "Good night, Matthew."

She stepped into the house, shutting the door quickly behind her. She lingered by the entrance, her heart pounding as she heard Matthew's footsteps come closer.

The steps stopped, and she closed her eyes tightly, willing him to leave. Then a few seconds later, she heard him thumping down the porch steps.

All was silent except for Samuel and Jared talking quietly in the living room.

She released a breath before heading to the kitchen to wait for dinner.

Wilma and Ada were talking while they cooked, and they didn't even notice her. Debbie must've been upstairs.

Krystal shook her head, thinking about what had just happened. What was wrong with Matthew? So often he'd made her feel like his last resort—his backup woman.

The last thing she wanted to be was someone's second choice, let alone a third choice.

He was a young, confused boy who wasn't quite yet a man. She needed a real man, someone like Jed. A smile danced around her lips as she thought about Jed.

The moment she'd laid eyes on Jed, she no longer

cared about Matthew. There was no comparison between the two men.

Jed had all the qualities that made her swoon: charismatic, amusing, non-judgmental, and open-minded. He was like herself in so many ways that all she could think about was when she would see him again. If what she had with him was real, she knew she'd be seeing him soon.

CHAPTER 15

*C*herish noticed how Jed looked a little depressed lately, so she invited Jed and Ruth for dinner, hoping he'd cheer up. He liked his food, and she and Favor spent half the day making his favorite crumbed, deep-fried chicken.

During the meal, Favor took an opportunity to talk about her best friend. "So, Jed. I hear you met my best friend, Krystal."

A smile curved on his lips, and he placed the drumstick he'd been munching down on his plate. "Yes. She told me about you and how she came to the community."

Favor was surprised by that. Krystal didn't usually tell people private things about herself. "So, do you like her?"

Jed's face took on a more serious expression. "Of course. She's the most extraordinary woman I've ever met. I can't stop thinking about her."

Favor was surprised to hear a man speak so candidly about his emotions; her eyebrows lifted in surprise. "Well, listen up. Since joining the community, things haven't been easy for her. She doesn't need someone who's playing games with her. She needs a serious man. Not serious, meaning that he's not humorous at times. She needs a guy who's serious about his relationship with her."

"It's good of you to watch out for your friend, but you don't have to be concerned about me. I care about her."

Favor felt a connection with Jed. She could envision how perfect he could be for Krystal. "Do it," she told him. "Go to her."

"What?"

"Just go and surprise her."

"Do you think so?" Jed rubbed his chin and looked at Ruth, who gave a nod of approval.

"Yes! What's the worst that could happen?" Favor asked.

"Ada did mention I was welcome to stay with her if I ever wanted to visit. I'll call her and ask if it's still okay."

"Well, then it's settled. What are you waiting for?" Cherish asked with a laugh.

Everyone stared at Jed, waiting for a response.

Jed stretched his frame to his full height as he stood up. "You're right. Ruth will be fine if I go for a few weeks."

"Hey, I can take care of myself. I've been doing that ever since my husband died."

"If I can take your car, Ruth, it will only take me a few hours to get there."

"Sure, you can take it. I'll drive the truck around until you get back," Ruth said.

Favor was taken aback. She had heard he drove a car, but never thought he'd admit it so openly. "You drive a car?"

Jed nodded. "I only drive when necessary. Why pay for a cab when I can drive myself? I don't have a horse and buggy here because I don't know how long I'll stay."

Malachi shook his head at his brother. "Sit down. You can't go anywhere right now, and you can't drive there. Just be normal for once, would you?"

Jed sank back onto the chair.

Favor grasped what Cherish meant when she said he was a rule breaker. And he didn't care who knew it. "Don't drive. You'll be talked about. Krystal needs a man who will do the right thing. She wants a proper Amish man, not one who is half in and half out. That's no good to her."

Jed rubbed his chin. "I'm all in. I just have my view of things."

Favor shook her head. "No. You must do what your community says. That's how Krystal wants to live. Can you do that? For Krystal?"

"I can do anything once I have a good reason. No problem. I could probably leave in a few days if I get everything sorted now," Jed said. "But you guys need workers at your house."

"Don't worry about the house. There are enough workers already," Simon told him.

Malachi chipped in with a joke. "Yeah, like you do any meaningful work anyway, Jed."

Jed smiled at his brother's comment. "Seems like everyone wants me gone. I do need to see her again."

Cherish nodded. "If that's what you want, go for it."

Jed declared, "All right then. I'm doing it."

"Then you'll have to book a car for the trip. If you truly want to win Krystal's heart, Jed, you need to do the right thing. Don't drive a car while you're there, use a horse and buggy. Be a proper Amish man." Ruth wagged her finger at him.

Jed laughed. "It'll be hard to be proper, but I'll do my best. She's worth it."

Simon reached for another chicken leg. "This is delicious. You have the recipe for this, don't you, Favor?"

Favor chuckled. "Of course I do. We can have that as often as you want. Every night if you want to, now we can make our own decisions about what we eat."

While the others discussed the recipe and talked about the yummy food, Jed was already thinking about seeing Krystal again. He couldn't wait to see her face light up when she saw him. He was ready to jump in and find out what would happen.

One day later, Jed set out on his journey to see Krystal. He had never felt so nervous in his whole life. The thought of seeing her was a mixture of excitement and fear. The enthusiasm that he might finally have a chance to confess his feelings and also he feared she might not feel the same way.

There was always a chance he might have been a holiday romance for her.

As he got closer, his palms sweated. He had rehearsed what he would say to her throughout the long drive, but now his mind had gone blank.

Finally, he arrived at Ada's place. He took a deep breath, then stepped out of the car.

CHAPTER 16

*D*ebbie was walking through the orchard toward Florence's house, munching on an apple. The late afternoon sun shone weakly creating dappled patterns on the grass while a light breeze rustled through the trees.

A sense of tranquility enveloped her, and she found her mind occupied by thoughts of Fritz. She was so excited for his return.

She dreamed of the day she and Fritz could stroll together, hand in hand, underneath the trees.

She pictured Jared and their future children racing and laughing around them as if it was already part of their daily routine to explore the orchard. This place had become her favorite spot in the world.

A thought of Peter crossed her mind, and she wondered how he was faring. She silently wished him well but realized it might be hard for him to understand why she chose to marry his brother after only a few months of knowing each other when she had been dating Peter for years and not accepting his proposals.

She could sympathize with the difficulty of that situation, yet she could never forgive him for breaking her trust. She was always unsure about Peter but was sure about everything with Fritz. She knew she could trust him like no other. Their connection was unlike anything she'd ever experienced before. It was love at first sight. She had always wondered if that was true, and now she knew it was.

All those years of being confused and worrying about her life with Peter had led her to become engaged to Fritz.

Everything happened the way God had designed it.

Approaching the back fence of Florence's house, Debbie could see Iris running around in the garden while Florence was sitting on the porch sipping tea. Carter was busy at work on the yard's far side, and Debbie gave him a polite wave as she moved nearer to the patio.

Florence saw her coming, stood up, and greeted her with an enthusiastic wave. "Debbie!"

Debbie hurried to sit down as she noticed how big Florence had gotten. "No, please don't stand on my account."

Florence settled herself back into her seat.

"I can't believe how much you've grown!" Debbie leaned over and patted her tummy.

Florence laughed. "I know—time passes so quickly. I feel like this pregnancy is going on forever, though."

"I should try to make more time to come see you; I apologize that I haven't been in a while."

"It's not a bother at all." Florence smiled as she watched Iris play with the dog in the garden. Debbie also looked out at the scenic orchard that made up their view and noticed how stunning it was with the sun producing a soft pink and violet light across the sky. "It's truly incredible up here. I've never realized until now," Debbie said.

"It's quite a sight, isn't it? I often sit here to watch the sun go down."

"It's gorgeous."

"Being the size I am, I can't do much else other than sit around." Florence placed her hand over her belly.

"You don't have long to go now."

"I know." Florence looked over at Debbie. "Are you doing alright?"

Debbie sighed loudly. "I'm well. I've been busy making preparations for the wedding."

"You must be so thrilled."

"I am."

"And what about the dresses?" Florence asked.

"Ada and Wilma offered to help me out."

Florence wrinkled her nose. "I could make them for you."

Debbie shook her head. "No, that's too much for you right now. It would be best if you took a break since you're pregnant. Plus, there's no rush on the wedding so far."

"That's beside the point. It's better to prepare in

advance. I am okay with sewing them as long as I start now. That way, they should be finished by the end of the year."

"I think it's too much for you."

"It's not. It will keep me occupied. Ada or Wilma can take over if I am too tired to finish."

"Only if you're positive about it."

"Absolutely." Florence smiled.

"But I haven't decided who my attendants will be yet."

"Why don't we start by taking your measurements, and then we can get started on your dress? That'll take the most time to make anyway."

Debbie was filled with gratitude for having Florence in her life. "Thanks a lot, Florence. I would love that."

"My pleasure. How is Wilma doing?"

Debbie smiled at the thought of Wilma and Obadiah locked in a gaze during Sunday service, oblivious to the rest of the congregation. "A new man has arrived. Krystal and I met him at the Sunday meeting. He used to live here. His name is Obadiah. Do you know him?"

Florence furrowed her brow. "I can't quite place him, but his name sounds familiar."

"He and Wilma must be more than just old friends."

"What makes you say that?"

"Let's just say I've never seen Wilma lost for words before."

Florence's laugh was muffled by her hand as she snickered. "Do you think she's in love?"

"I think so."

"That's so sweet! I can't wait to meet him."

"I'm sure you will soon. He's very nice and he seems kind. It's what she needs."

"I wonder if I'll get along with him. I never really got along with Levi."

"I didn't know," Debbie said.

"It's true. I know he's your uncle, but we never really saw eye to eye. We tolerated each other, and that was all."

For an hour or so, the ladies stayed outside on the porch, chatting and laughing. After that, Florence ushered Debbie in to take measurements for her wedding dress.

CHAPTER 17

 rystal was working in the back of her shop, organizing fabric swatches, when she heard the front doorbell. Instantly, she stood up and adjusted her *kapp* and apron, before proceeding to the front of the store.

A tall figure with his back turned to her was near the entrance. When the man turned around, Krystal's heart leaped.

"Jed!" She blinked, making sure she wasn't dreaming. Jed smiled and started walking toward her. Krystal was in complete shock. "What are you doing here?"

"I've come to see you. Why else would I be here?" He leaned against the counter that separated them.

"I wasn't expecting to see you so soon."

"I wanted to surprise you."

He looked so good with his tanned skin and hazel eyes. "I'm so pleased you came."

"Good. That makes two of us. Can I take you out on a date, Miss?" he inquired.

Giggling, Krystal covered her mouth. "So formal. I'd love that, but I can't go right now. How long are you here for? Where are you staying?"

"I could be here for a couple of weeks. I'm staying with Ada and Samuel. Ada said we're going to your place for the evening meal tonight."

Krystal was dumbfounded; Ada had kept this from her. They both had, but she wasn't mad about that.

"So this is your quilt store, hey?" Jed looked around the store.

"This is it," Krystal said proudly.

"Your quilts are beautiful. Do you make them all?"

"Most of them are on consignment."

"I'd love to purchase one for myself."

Krystal couldn't keep the smile from her face. "You don't have to do that. I'll make you one."

"No." He shook his head. "It's too much work. Maybe you could make us both one if things work out between us."

Krystal felt her cheeks burn as she looked deeply into his hazel eyes. She had no words. It was delightful to like someone who liked her back. This romance could go somewhere.

"So, are you glad I'm here?" Jed leaned in toward her.

Krystal was captivated by his eyes, but the sound of the doorbell jingling snapped her out of it. She stood upright ready to greet the customer, but it was no customer.

It was Matthew, and he had two take-out cups in his hands.

"Matthew? What are you doing here?" Krystal blurted out. He had the worst timing in the world.

Jed turned around to face Matthew.

The smile on Matthew's face faded as he looked from one to the other, as though he was working out what was going on. "I've brought you coffee like I always do."

"I didn't ask for coffee. I'm sorry, I don't want it." Krystal frowned. He hadn't brought her coffee in months. Why did he phrase it like that?

"I'm Jed. Nice to meet you," Jed held out his hand for Matthew to shake. Matthew set a cup of coffee in front of Krystal before clasping Jed's hand.

"You're Jed?"

"Correct. That's what I said."

"I don't believe I've seen you around here before. Are you here on vacation?" Matthew pulled his shoulders back and stood tall, but he still didn't reach Jed's height.

"I'm here to see Krystal."

Matthew raised his eyebrows, and a thick silence filled the room. Krystal could feel the tension growing by the second. She knew she had to say something to end the awkwardness. "Jed is Malachi's brother. He's from Willersburg."

"Well, most recently, I'm from Willersburg. I don't

stay too long in one place, but I'm looking to change that soon." Jed looked over at Krystal and smiled.

Matthew looked at Krystal. "So you met him when you visited Cherish?"

"That's right," Jed said. "Anyway, Krystal. I have to go back to Ada's and take care of some things there, so when would you like me to take you on a date?"

Krystal smiled brightly at Jed. "I'll see if Bliss can work here tomorrow. We could spend the day together."

"I'd love that," replied Jed.

"You're staying at my aunt's place?" Matthew inquired.

"Ada Berger's your aunt?"

"Yes."

"That's where I'm staying."

"Wow!" Matthew hung his head.

"Is there a problem?" Jed snapped.

Matthew appeared to shrink away. "No, no problem," he answered weakly.

"Well then, nice to meet you, Matthew. Krystal, I'll see you tonight. Oh, you said you didn't want this coffee, Krystal?"

"No!"

"I'll have it." He grabbed the takeout cup and walked to the door while taking a sip. "Nice. Thanks for this, Martin."

"It's Matthew."

When Jed reached the door, he turned and gave Krystal a dazzling smile before leaving.

She beamed until she felt Matthew staring at her with complete disapproval.

"What a performance that was. Is he always like that?" Matthew's lips turned down at the corners.

"Yes."

"So, it looks like you were telling the truth," Matthew remarked. "I wasn't sure if you were deceiving me like you deceived me with Sigrid."

"I told you about Jed. I'm not hiding anything. I know I was wrong to do the whole Sigrid thing, but it showed me your true colors. I'm not sorry about that part."

"I found out what you did is called entrapment." Matthew took a mouthful of coffee. Then he murmured, "I can't believe he took the coffee."

"What are you going on about, Matthew?"

"I think you know. Anyway, you've made up your mind. This guy must be serious if he's come all this way to see you. Are you sure about him?"

"I keep telling you, we're done, Matthew. Who I'm sure about or not sure about has nothing to do with you."

"So, you're saying you're not sure about him?"

Krystal was far beyond simply angry with him. She was now anxious Jed would think she liked Matthew if he kept hanging around. "I am sure."

"What's so great about him, huh? He doesn't seem like a nice guy. He barely said hello. He didn't want to get to know me, and he took the coffee I bought for you."

Krystal shot Matthew an exasperated look. "Really, Matthew? That upset you?"

"What do you know about him?" he shot back.

"What does it matter? I thought I knew you, but obviously, I didn't."

Matthew stared at the ground, seeming completely lost, but Krystal had no sympathy. "I'm sorry, Matthew. But I don't think you were particularly nice to Jed just now. Remember, he is Malachi's brother."

"Me? I'm always nice. He was the one—"

"I think it's time to leave, Matthew. I'll see you around, I'm sure." Krystal walked into her back room to continue sorting through her fabrics.

When she heard the doorbell chime, she was relieved Matthew was gone. Now she could think about Jed. She couldn't believe he was here and she couldn't wait to tell Debbie and the others!

CHAPTER 18

*C*herish and Favor painted walls at Favor and Simon's house while the men worked. So far, the kitchen and living room were the only completed rooms. Favor had decided to paint the living room a soft shade of lemon.

At any moment, Simon and Favor's housewarming gift would arrive.

Cherish couldn't wait to see their faces when they saw their new couch. It was a perfect gift for their new home.

Cherish felt guilty about buying brand new things for herself and only thought it fair they help Simon and Favor. It was the least they could do to thank them for moving to be close to them.

After all, she knew how hard it was for Simon to move away from his parents. Cherish wanted to make life as comfortable as possible for them, and now that they had the money to do so, she saw nothing wrong with helping out her family.

Favor stood on a small ladder finishing the final touches of paint in the corner of the living room. When she was done, she stood beside Cherish, who had just finished the section she'd been working on.

"Well, what do you think?" Favor asked as they stepped back to observe their work.

"This is lovely!" Cherish said with delight as she admired their handiwork.

"It looks like a dream come true!" Favor scanned the room again, this time with tears in her eyes.

Cherish noticed and put an arm around her shoulder. "What's wrong?"

"I'm just so grateful to be away from Simon's parents." Favor cried as she spoke, making Cherish giggle uncontrollably. She embraced Favor tightly, and they both laughed.

"What are you two laughing at?" Simon asked as he entered with Malachi in tow.

"Nothing," Cherish said.

Malachi's gaze darted around the room. "It looks great in here!"

Simon noticed Favor was upset and went to comfort her. "What's wrong?"

"They're happy tears. She's just happy to be here." Cherish walked over and leaned on Malachi, who in turn put his arm around her shoulders.

"We made fresh lemonade. I'll fetch some for us." Favor grabbed the jug of lemonade and poured it into cups for everyone. Before they finished drinking their lemonade, a knock sounded on the door.

"Who can that be?" Simon frowned in confusion as the workers usually just walked in and out of the house without knocking.

Malachi merely shrugged as Cherish placed her glass down before quickly running past Simon to answer it. "I'll go." Cherish opened the door to find Sam from the store.

"Couch delivery!" Sam boomed in a loud voice.

Favor stepped beside her and replied, "No, you must have the wrong address. We didn't order anything."

"Yes, we did! Thanks," Cherish said as Sam turned and headed to his van to unload the couch.

"Wait, what?" Simon asked.

"Happy housewarming present!" Cherish said.

Favor's mouth fell open. "You got us a couch?"

"Yes! I saw it in the store and had to get it for you two. It'll look great here!"

Cherish's kindness overwhelmed Favor, who enveloped her in a hug.

"Cherish and Malachi, it's far too kind of you," Simon said as he and Malachi moved past them to help the man carry the couch.

Once the couch had been placed in the living room, Cherish and Favor sat on it excitedly, talking a mile a minute.

"This is the most marvelous couch I have ever sat on!" Favor rubbed her hands over the fabric. "I'll have to put a cover on it to keep it nice."

"Thank you very much, Malachi and Cherish. This is a delightful gift," Simon said quietly.

Malachi looked over at Cherish. "It was Cherish's idea."

Cherish could detect slight annoyance in her husband's voice, but the others wouldn't have noticed.

KRYSTAL GOT out of bed and slipped into her favorite dress before weaving her hair into a braid and placing her prayer *kapp* on top. She was so excited to spend today with Jed. She ran down the stairs and into the kitchen, grinning from ear to ear.

As she approached the kitchen, she was surprised to hear Jed's voice among the voices that sounded from the kitchen.

Ada, Wilma, and Debbie were preparing breakfast while Samuel chatted casually with Jed at the table. Jared was alone at his children's table.

It made sense that Jed was there since he was staying with Ada and Samuel. She gave him a friendly smile, and he winked at her in response as she entered the kitchen.

"Good morning, everybody! Is there anything I can do to help?" Krystal offered.

"We're almost done, Krystal. Have a seat at the table," Ada said before setting down a bowl of scrambled eggs in the center.

"You look very nice today," Debbie remarked as she sat beside Krystal.

"Thank you! I'm looking forward to the day!" Krystal replied happily.

"Likewise," Jed grinned at Krystal, who struggled to control the smile that crept onto her face as soon as their eyes locked.

She felt like a teenager again, and it was all thanks to him. Ada deftly moved a tower of toast beside the scrambled eggs before finding her seat next to Samuel. Wilma followed, placing bacon and sausages on the table before sitting beside Ada. After saying a quick and silent prayer of gratitude for their meal, they started eating.

"What are you two planning for today?" Ada inquired.

Krystal smiled at Jed before responding. "I was thinking maybe we could tour the town and visit you at the markets, Debbie."

"That would be nice. I'm sure Jed will enjoy the markets. I look forward to seeing both of you."

"Can I join too?" Jared pleaded.

"No, honey, you have school today." Debbie took a bite of toast.

"Aww! That's not fair!" he groaned in reply.

"The teacher said you're the smartest in your class, Jared!" Ada blurted out.

"Wow!" he exclaimed, and Debbie inwardly grimaced, hoping he wouldn't retell that to the other students. "That means I can have a day off while the others catch up."

Samuel chuckled loudly. "I'm afraid it doesn't work like that, Jared."

Jared pouted.

Wilma then asked Debbie, "Anything new from Fritz?"

Debbie cast her gaze downward and stirred her food around with her fork. "No, nothing yet."

Ada suggested, "Maybe you should reach out to him and ask for a date for the wedding. I know you don't want to pressure him, but these things take planning, and we need to know how much time we have." As she spoke, Ada cut her toast into four pieces.

"I agree," Debbie replied, despite feeling uneasy. Nevertheless, she couldn't stop worrying about why he hadn't set an appropriate date.

"Ada and I have been experimenting with cake recipes," Wilma said around a mouthful of food.

"*Jah*, we are going to make our favorites for you to try soon," Ada responded, spreading butter evenly on each of the four pieces of toast.

"Can I try the cake too? Please?" Jared begged. "I can tell you which ones are good."

"Of course, you can." Wilma nodded.

"If you're a good boy, you can try them with me and help me decide which ones to serve at the wedding. You can be my taste tester." Debbie looked lovingly at Jared, whose eyes grew wide in anticipation of such an honor.

"Yay! I'll be so good, *Mamm!*"

"I'm glad to hear it," Debbie grinned happily at her son. She was incredibly grateful someone had come into Jared's life that could understand and adore him just as much as she did. The fact Jared felt the same way about Fritz brought her even more joy; within a few months, he had become closer to Fritz than he had been with Peter in years.

"I wonder how Favor and Simon are settling in," Samuel said.

"Jed, tell us. How do they seem to be getting on?" Ada asked.

"They seem to be settling in well from what I've seen. Their house is coming along nicely."

"The place wasn't much, but it would still be better than staying with Simon's folks." Wilma spoke quietly, hoping no one would catch her comment.

"Wilma, that's not very kind," Ada chided.

"Oh gosh! Did I say that out loud?" Wilma glanced around in confusion, causing Debbie and Krystal to giggle at the two older ladies.

"A visit to Favor and Simon's house when it's finished would be wonderful," Samuel suggested. "I know you and Wilma will want to see it."

"Oh yes! I completely agree!" Ada nodded enthusiastically.

"What a great plan. Can I go too, *Mamm?*" Jared asked.

Debbie chuckled. "Not right away, but we will go

soon. We will plan a trip after the wedding. Before that, I'll have too much to do."

Ada stared at Jared. "Give the adults a chance to talk, Jared."

Jared slouched in his chair and continued eating.

"So, Jed. Tell us about Malachi. Why weren't any of your family at the wedding?" Ada asked out of the blue, causing Wilma to almost choke on the food in her mouth.

An uncomfortable quiet took over the room until Jed finished eating. "I think those questions are ones you should be asking Malachi, not me."

"We'll never get anything out of him." Ada shook her head and went back to eating.

Jed glanced over at Krystal and gave her a mischievous wink, which sent a flurry of excitement through her.

CHAPTER 19

*A*da and Wilma busied themselves with tidying after breakfast as the others made their way out for the day. Jed guided Krystal to the horse and buggy he'd borrowed from Samuel and opened the buggy door for her.

Krystal felt a flutter in her chest; he was so polite! Even though he'd only been there briefly, she already enjoyed his company. Now she had to hope that he'd be able to see himself living in this town.

Jed sat beside her and closed his buggy door. "Where to?"

"Would you like me to show you the park before we go to the markets? It's got a lake in the center. You can usually spot baby ducks there, too," she said.

He chuckled at her suggestion. "Who could say no to baby ducks?" He clicked his tongue to get the horse moving.

The sun shone brightly as they drove along, and

birds chirped above them, creating a tranquil atmosphere. When they reached the park, Jed was captivated by the sight of vast green grass stretching out before them and tall trees encircling the area, making it seem more isolated than it was.

They got out of the buggy and he secured the horse to a hitching post. Then they started walking. "Wow," was all he could say when he saw the lake.

"It's beautiful, isn't it? I come here sometimes to clear my thoughts and be with God."

"I'm going to come here every day when I live here."

Krystal smiled hopefully, praying he meant it when he said he wanted to move here for her. He was mature and authoritative, giving off a sense of security Matthew could never have managed. When they reached the banks of the lake, they stood side by side, marveling at its beauty.

"It's calming, don't you think?" Krystal asked.

"It's almost as stunning as you," Jed responded, turning to meet her gaze. Krystal felt her heart racing as their eyes locked together. "I'm so glad I met you, Krystal."

"Me too." They smiled at each other until quacking ducks interrupted the moment. "Look! There they are!" Krystal squealed with delight when she spotted them. A mother duck swam slowly along the water, trailing six little ducklings behind it.

"They are adorable." Jed chuckled. "You know, this town is much better than Malachi's in terms of what I've seen so far."

"You really think that?" Krystal stood up straighter as she waited for Jed's reply.

"Yeah. I relate to the people better. I particularly like Ada, and Samuel is so wise with his few words. He doesn't say much, but when he speaks, it's meaningful."

Krystal smiled, glad he liked the place. "Everyone here is so kind. I feel fortunate to call them my family."

As they strolled around the lake, Jed inquired, "Do you mind if I ask what led you to become Amish?"

"It's a long story. I've told you most of it already."

"Tell me again."

She gave a little laugh. "I came as Favor's penpal. She didn't tell her folks I was coming, so I just showed up. But I wasn't really her pen pal. I had been impersonating Favor's pen pal. Her real pen pal was my best friend, who died in a horrible accident. Her parents blamed me, but it wasn't my fault. That's why I had to get away. Caroline, my friend, had always been telling me she wanted to stay with Favor. I had no money, no place to go, so I wrote and told Favor I was coming."

"What about your mother?"

"She worked for Caroline's parents as a maid. She was kicked out, too, after Caroline died. She moved up north, and I went to visit Favor."

"It's an amazing story."

"I was deceptive back then."

"From what you say, it was out of desperation. It's an awful thing to have no place you can call home."

Krystal knew he was talking about himself. He was staying with Ruth. "From there, it took me a while to gain the family's trust when they found out I lied about who I was. I moved with my mom for a while, and then I came back. They took me back. It was hard for me to believe they could forgive and forget. It made me search my heart. I wanted to be forgiving and kind like them. That's why I ended up joining their community. I never knew I wouldn't be accepted as one of them."

"You're not accepted?"

"Not really."

Jed shook his head. "Who cares what they think, right? It's God who matters, and He accepts you."

She smiled up at him. "I know, but I have to live in this world, and it would make it easier if I felt more fully Amish."

He chuckled. "Don't worry about it. You have people around you who love you. They treat you like you're family."

"I know. I'm very blessed in that regard. Now I think about it, I should be more grateful for everything I have. I inherited the quilt store. Did you know that?"

"No. You never told me."

"I worked for an old lady, and she died. I found out she'd left me the quilt store."

"You must've meant a lot to her."

Krystal nodded. "We were close. I feel her every day when I walk into the store. Is that weird?"

"No. It must be comforting."

"It is, in a way." After talking to Jed, Krystal felt an even deeper connection with him. He was incredibly understanding and caring toward her.

As they kept walking, he interlaced his fingers with hers; when she looked up at him, a tingly feeling in the pit of her stomach spread through her whole body.

Suddenly her gaze shifted forward, narrowing in shock as she spotted a familiar figure standing beneath a tree. It was Matthew and he was waving at them.

What on earth is he doing here?

How did he know they were going to be at the park today? She recalled he had been in her store when they were talking about a date, and here they were. They'd never said they were going to the park or even when they'd be there.

Noticing Jed was looking down and hadn't seen Matthew, she spun around. "Let's go back."

Jed raised an eyebrow, confused by her hasty action, but followed along obediently. She was positive Jed would assume something suspicious was happening if he caught sight of Matthew for a second time.

She had tried as hard as possible to make her wishes clear to Matthew, so why wouldn't he leave her alone?

"You feeling alright, Krystal?"

"Yes. It's getting chilly out. Let's go back to the buggy, and I'll show you the markets now, okay?"

"Sure thing."

The ride to the market was short; all Krystal could do was stare at Jed, not quite believing he'd come to see her.

When they reached the markets, they parked the buggy in the shade before walking over to Debbie's stall. When they arrived, they waited until Debbie finished with a customer before saying hello.

"Welcome!" Debbie greeted them cheerfully.

Jed admired the teas, all lined up in brightly colored boxes. "This is a lovely store you have here, Debbie. Do you make all these teas by yourself?"

"I did, but now I have a packing center to help with the demand."

Krystal added, "She also sells online."

"Yes. Krystal helped me with the website, and she also ships the packages for me. Here, this one is for you." Debbie leaned down and grabbed a gift bag, passing it to Jed. "This is a special bag I put together for you. It contains herbal teas that are great for relieving various ailments. They're all labeled so you know which one to use for sleep, headaches, and other issues."

"Thank you very much, Debbie!" Jed said as he took the bag from her. He was enjoying this new community; everyone had been so friendly and welcoming compared to other places he'd been before.

"I can't get enough of Debbie's teas. I drink them every day."

"I can't wait to taste them for myself." He peeped into the bag. "Thanks again."

Debbie noticed Krystal and Jed gazing lovingly at each other as if they were the only two people in the world. It reminded her how she felt when she looked at Fritz. She was thankful; after all their struggles with relationships, it seemed like they'd both found suitable men.

Once they had parted ways with Debbie, Jed and Krystal continued to explore the marketplace. Before leaving, they stopped to enjoy a meal at one of the food carts.

On their way out, Krystal noticed Matthew, who was supposed to be working at the orchard. There was no way this was a coincidence.

He was following them!

This was weird. Fury bubbled up inside her once again, and she quickly pulled Jed toward an ice cream stand so he wouldn't see Matthew.

"You've got to try this ice cream. It's delicious," she said.

"I love ice cream."

"Me too."

CHAPTER 20

*A*fter finishing seeing Krystal at the farmers markets with another man, Matthew knew what to do—talk with Fairfax. He always gave him good advice. Since Fairfax was his boss, he'd have to explain why he had taken a day off. It would put him behind schedule, but he could make up for it by doing longer hours in the coming days.

Matthew made his way into the orchard and spotted Fairfax working near a fence. Without wasting any time, Matthew strode up to him.

"Fairfax," Matthew said firmly, "I need your help."

Fairfax placed his shovel down and took off his work gloves. "It's always nice to see you, Matthew. Did you forget you're supposed to show up for work at six?"

"I'm sorry, but I had to take a personal day. I'll make up the time."

Fairfax frowned at him. "Are you ill?"

Matthew shook his head.

Fairfax noticed he didn't seem himself. "What's wrong?"

Matthew feared Fairfax would be upset at him, but he needed advice from someone. As well as being his boss, Fairfax had become like an older brother. "I've been trailing Krystal around."

"Following her?"

"I prefer to say trailing. She's got some new companion."

Fairfax made a sound of acknowledgment as he scratched his neck. "How do you feel about that?"

"I'm certain there was something genuine between us, and it doesn't seem as serious with her current beau. They appear to be quite close when they're in each other's company, yet Krystal and I go back a long way, whereas this guy is more of a recent addition. She wouldn't have time to grow feelings for this guy, so I need your advice on how to get her to forget this guy."

"I think it's best to let Krystal go," Fairfax said. "Trust is hard to rebuild once it's been broken."

"Do you think so?"

Fairfax slowly nodded. "You need to move on from Krystal. She's found someone else, so maybe you must look around for someone more suited to you."

Matthew was quiet for a moment before asking, "How is Sigrid doing? Is she still around, or has she gone home?"

"She's still here. I'm sure you saw her at the Sunday meeting, *jah?*"

"Yeah, but I thought she might have gone home after the meeting."

"Are you back to being interested in Sigrid now?"

Matthew gave a shrug and then nodded.

Fairfax let out a long, heavy sigh. "The way I see it, you don't want to make her feel like an afterthought. But that's exactly how she feels, and I can't blame her."

Matthew furrowed his brow in thought. "So, you're saying there's still hope with Sigrid?"

"I'm not sure about that," Fairfax replied, shaking his head. "You'll have to talk to her yourself. But you should try to move on from Krystal and let her be happy. You've broken her trust more than once."

"Ah, I see. So, I haven't completely destroyed Sigrid's trust in me—I've only made her mad. That's it! Now everything is clear. Can you do me a favor?"

Fairfax hesitated. He did not want to be responsible for pushing Matthew back toward Sigrid. "I guess so, depending on what the favor is."

Matthew then took a pen and a handkerchief from his pocket and wrote Sigrid a note before presenting it to Fairfax. "Can you please deliver this to Sigrid for me?"

Fairfax looked at the handkerchief that looked as though it had fallen into the dirt. He ran his fingers through his hair in thought before he took it from him. "Sure, I'll give it to her, but I wouldn't get your hopes too high, considering how badly you hurt her."

"I appreciate it." He looked up at the sun. "I'll do a couple of hours work before we lose the daylight."

"Good."

Fairfax headed home at the end of his work day. As he entered the kitchen and approached Hope, she told him the evening meal was almost ready. Fairfax thanked her and planted a kiss on her cheek before handing the note over to Sigrid, who was helping with the meal. "Here you are, Sigrid. I have a kind of a letter from Matthew for you."

Sigrid took the handkerchief from him. She furrowed her brow as she examined it, confused as to why Matthew would want her to have it. When she opened, she saw the scrawled writing. *'Sigrid, meet me at the park at noon Saturday. Matthew.'*

Hope and Fairfax stared at Sigrid. "What are you planning to do?" Hope inquired.

Sigrid stomped over to the kitchen table and sat on a chair. "Why won't he just leave me alone?" A tear trickled down her cheek.

Fairfax exited to get ready for dinner while Hope came over and sat beside her friend. "Try not to let him emotionally affect you," Hope said gently. "I'm sure he's trying to make up for his past mistakes."

"It's too late," Sigrid barked. "He was so mean to me."

"Do you still have any feelings for him?" Hope questioned sympathetically.

Sigrid shook her head sadly. "I thought I did, but no, I don't think so. Not now."

"Go to the park, then. Tell him you're through and to leave you alone."

Sigrid wiped her eyes. "You're right. I'll go to the park and confront him. It won't be easy, but it has to be done."

CHAPTER 21

*W*hen Friday evening rolled around, Krystal was mashing potatoes alongside Debbie in the kitchen. Ada and Wilma were busy prepping other dishes for Adam's birthday dinner. Krystal was disappointed Jed wasn't going to be there.

Ada had informed her that Jed was exhausted and had been having trouble sleeping. Krystal hoped it wasn't a sign of something more serious.

Bliss had come early to help with the preparations, and she was delicately finishing decorating the cake she'd made. The cake was in the shape of a giant bunny with two tiny bunnies on each side.

Debbie saw the cake and couldn't believe it. "Oh my, that's the most adorable cake I've ever seen!"

"I hope Adam appreciates my work," Bliss said with a chuckle. "I had to make a huge cake and then create the shape. Our love of rabbits brought us together."

Ada overheard their conversation. "He probably

meant he likes eating them, *jah?*" Ada snickered. "If I had known everyone was following a theme tonight, I would have made a rabbit stew."

Bliss wasn't amused by the joke and shook her head as Ada continued cooking.

"Are you nervous about seeing Matthew tonight?" Debbie asked Krystal in a hushed tone while they mashed potatoes together.

Krystal trembled. "Seeing Sigrid and Matthew in one room will be uncomfortable. I didn't realize he was coming. He's not, is he?"

"He might show up if he hears about it. He's so used to coming to all our family dinners," Wilma said.

"I know." Krystal nodded.

"It ought to be okay; you're all grown-ups," Ada responded. "It won't be awkward unless you make it that way."

"Does he know about the dinner?" Wilma queried, looking at Ada.

"I haven't seen him."

"So, he's not going to show up?" Krystal asked.

"I didn't extend an invitation either," Bliss replied as she continued adorning her cake.

"I guess we're in the clear," Debbie said with relief.

Ada giggled, holding her belly. "It wouldn't have worked, would it? We couldn't match Sigrid up with Andrew if Matthew's in the same room. No, that simply wouldn't do."

Krystal and Debbie exchanged glances, surprised

and amused by Ada's change of attitude. She was normally trying to match Matthew.

Once the dinner guests had arrived, Ada invited them all into the room off from the kitchen, where a long table was set for the meal.

One after another, they made their way through the entryway, and Ada directed them to their chairs.

"Obadiah, make your way over to Samuel. You can sit next to him," Ada said as Obadiah wandered into the room. They had decided to invite Obadiah and Eli to the dinner rather than have them on Thursday night as previously arranged.

Ada continued telling people where to sit. "Wilma, you join me at the other end of the table. Sigrid, why don't you sit next to Andrew?"

Andrew looked up and smiled at Sigrid as she sat down.

When everyone was seated, Ada took her place at the table before they all bowed their heads in prayer to give thanks for the food.

Ada opened her eyes, and a feeling of satisfaction washed over her, knowing she had successfully seated Andrew and Sigrid beside each other without arousing suspicion. She glanced at the food spread across the table, and her mouth watered at the sight of the roast pork and chicken drumsticks beside a large bowl of macaroni cheese and pasta salad.

According to Bliss, this was all of Adam's favorite dishes.

Ada filled a plate as she listened in to Sigrid and Andrew's conversation.

"I don't believe we've ever officially been introduced. I'm Andrew Weeks." He smiled, extending a hand for Sigrid to shake.

"I do know who you are. I'm Sigrid," she replied.

"It's great to meet you," Andrew said as he filled his plate. "You're from out of town, right?"

"I am."

"Will you be heading back home soon?"

Sigrid shrugged her shoulders. "I'm not sure. Maybe. I don't have any definite plans."

Andrew glanced around the table, noticing that everyone had stopped talking to listen in on their exchange. As Sigrid looked up, it was as if they'd been caught out. In an instant, everyone quickly started talking among themselves.

"So, what do you like to do for fun?" Sigrid asked.

"I enjoy harness racing."

"You can't be serious!" Sigrid turned fully to face Andrew. "My father used to take me to the races all the time. I would always go with him. It was a special thing we did together. I wasn't in the community then, and neither was my father, but there were Amish people there, and he raced against them."

Ada surreptitiously jabbed Wilma under the table with her foot.

"Ow!" Wilma exclaimed loudly, causing everyone at the table to look her way. "Oh, sorry. My back's hurting a bit today." Wilma shrugged it off before shooting Ada a glare.

After a moment, Andrew resumed talking with Sigrid. "That's incredible! I will be competing this weekend if you'd like to cheer me on."

"Really?" Sigrid asked before suddenly realizing the whole table was silently observing them again. She frowned at everyone and then looked back at Andrew and beamed him a smile. "I'd love that."

"Samuel could take you there, but who would bring you back?" Ada asked Sigrid.

"Yes, I can take you there, no problem," Samuel added.

"I could drive you home afterward," Andrew offered. "That is if you don't mind waiting around until I finish. It might be late."

"That sounds great. I don't mind waiting at all. I love the atmosphere of the races and being around the horses and all."

Ada muttered, "It's a date!" Everyone stared at Ada. She didn't seem to mind. "Eat up, everyone. There's plenty for everyone to have seconds."

Fairfax cleared his throat. "Wilma, Krystal said you saw a dog in the orchard."

"I did. Have you come across it?"

"No, but I'll keep an eye out."

"Poor thing. We'll have to rescue it if it's a stray," Debbie said.

Knowing Obadiah was a dog lover, Wilma nodded. "Oh yes. We will."

Ada eyed her suspiciously. "Do you mean you'd want to keep the dog, Wilma?"

Wilma gulped. "Naturally, I'd try to find the owner first."

"There are shelters around for that," Ada announced. "They locate the owners of lost dogs."

"You miss your daughter's dog, don't you, Wilma?" Obadiah asked.

"Oh yes."

Everyone stared at Wilma. Those who were close to her knew she didn't care for animals.

"I'll make an effort to take a look around the orchard tomorrow and see if I can find it," Fairfax said.

"Thank you, Fairfax." Wilma silently prayed that the dog had gone. The last thing she wanted was a pet. Now she was focused on Obadiah, who had started a conversation with Samuel.

"I'll swing by tomorrow and repair the balcony rail if that'll be okay with Wilma. I noticed it's a bit loose," Obadiah told Samuel. "Is that okay, Wilma?"

"Thank you. I'd be ever so grateful," Wilma said.

Samuel nodded. "I saw that earlier. I'll come too, and we can work on it together. I know where the tools are kept."

It's another date! Ada yelled in her mind. She'd made two successful matches tonight. One was for Sigrid, and the other was for a new friendship for Samuel. Ada looked over at Wilma, who kept gazing at Obadiah as though he was the best thing since heaters in buggies. Ada couldn't help but chuckle at her friend's obvious infatuation. If Obadiah checked out as suitable, it would be a relief to see Wilma happy after what she'd been through the past few years.

As the dinner progressed, the conversations became livelier, and Ada felt a sense of contentment wash over her. She had brought her loved ones together. Bliss had outdone herself with the dessert, a warm apple pie that had everyone raving. The bunny cake had caused a few laughs, too.

"Isn't the cake adorable?" Debbie remarked.

"Can I have some cake too? I love cake," Jared pleaded. "I love rabbits too. And dogs. Can I play with the dog if you can find it, Aunt Wilma?'

"Of course, but there's not much chance of that happening. I only saw it once."

"*Mamm,* what about the cake?" Jared asked.

"Only a little piece after you finish what's on your plate."

Jared turned his attention to eating.

At the end of the meal, Adam looked around the table at everyone. "Thank you, everyone, for tonight. It means a lot that you'd come together and do all this just for me."

"We were delighted to do it," Wilma said and everyone agreed.

Once the guests had left, Krystal, Debbie, Ada, and Wilma convened in the kitchen to clean up.

"Tonight was a huge success," Ada said, wiping the counter.

"We did great," Wilma agreed, putting away the dishes.

"What's going on? You've been quiet all night," Debbie said to Krystal.

"I'm alright. I'm happy Sigrid and Andrew seemed to get along well. Who could've seen that coming?"

Ada spun around. "We did. That was the whole idea of the night."

"I guess I'm just missing Jed," Krystal replied sadly. "He would've enjoyed tonight."

"I understand. I miss Fritz every day. Men have their own way of handling things; they can go months without talking while us women need more frequent communication," Debbie said.

Krystal sighed. "That's true. Are you worried about Fritz in any way?"

Debbie denied her worries with a shake of her head. She wished this conversation was in private. "A bit, but I need to be patient. Look at how Malachi waited for Cherish through all those years. We had no idea they were even together!"

"That's true. These matters take time, I guess," Krystal replied. "But he won't let you down. He's not that kind of man."

Debbie smiled at Krystal and gave her a nod.

CHAPTER 22

*T*he next day was Saturday, and Jed had recovered from his tiredness. He and Krystal had their minds set on another stroll around the park. Bliss was working in the quilt store today so Krystal could spend the whole day with Jed.

Jed was grateful he was staying at Ada's; he got to see Krystal often, seeing that Ada and Samuel practically lived at Wilma's house. He found it amusing how Ada was there nearly every day, and they ate most of their meals there.

In the short time he'd been there, everyone had grown on him, making his time enjoyable. He glanced at Krystal and felt comfortable enough to hold her hand. She simply gazed up at him and smiled. It all felt so normal. Nothing was forced or awkward between them.

They strolled around the glimmering lake in quiet contemplation. Krystal envisioned a future where she and Jed were married, with children filling their lives with joyous laughter. The mere thought of having her own kids brought a wave of anticipation throughout her body. She couldn't help but think about spending the rest of her life with Jed and wanted clarity about their future without being too eager. "I have a question for you."

"Sure. Ask away."

"Don't feel like I'm putting any pressure on you or anything, but can you tell me what the future of our relationship looks like?"

"Oh..."

Krystal was worried when Jed seemed taken aback by the question she had asked. "I just mean, we live in different places, and you mentioned moving here before, so now you've been here in person, what are your thoughts about moving here?"

Jed stopped walking and faced her directly. "It doesn't matter where I live. It never has. I'd move anywhere for you without hesitation."

"For real?" Krystal asked, her voice wavering.

"Yes, for real." He gave her hand a squeeze.

Krystal was overjoyed; she finally understood why everything with Matthew hadn't worked out. He couldn't compare to Jed when it came to her affections. He didn't even come close.

Looking into the distance she saw a lone figure. When she focused on the person, she saw it was Matthew. He was seated at the water's edge. Her anger flared in an instant. What was he doing here now, stalking them like this, and how did he know where they'd be again?

"What's wrong?" Jed followed her gaze and saw Matthew.

"Matthew is stalking us!"

Jed furrowed his brow. "Are you sure he's following us?"

"Positive," Krystal huffed. "I saw him here the first time we came, and then he followed us to the market."

Jed found her frustration endearing and a smile hinted around his lips.

Krystal looked up at him. "It's really not funny."

"You're cute when you're mad." He chuckled.

"This is serious. Matthew's trying to cling to something that doesn't exist anymore. I'm going to confront him."

She started walking, but he didn't let go of her hand. "Don't do that," he said.

Krystal turned to face Jed. "Why not?"

"You don't need to. What does it matter if he follows us? Let's not let it ruin our day. When he sees we're not bothered by him, I'm sure he'll lose interest. I think he's just trying to get you to notice him."

Krystal huffed. "He is unpredictable. Matthew's not like an ordinary person. He's got problems. I have to set boundaries."

"Alright, I'll wait here."

Krystal marched up to Matthew and when she reached him, she placed her hands on her hips.

Matthew sat bolt upright when he spotted her. "Krystal, what are you doing? Did you track me here?"

Krystal's mouth fell open. "Me, follow you? Are you kidding me?"

"What's going on?" Matthew stared at her as though he was waiting for her to explain herself.

"I saw you tailing us the other day, and now you've shown up again. Understand this, it's over between us. I am in love with Jed, and it is time for you to move on and forget me."

Matthew rose to his feet. "Wow. Love is a big word. I'm not here for you. I'm waiting for Sigrid."

Krystal stepped back but realized he was most likely making up stories. "Sure, you are," she said, full of sarcasm. "Why don't you start being real, Matthew? Sigrid is interested in Andrew Weeks, so she's not coming here to see you."

Before Matthew could respond, Krystal saw someone approaching.

It was Sigrid.

Krystal quickly spun around to avoid being seen by Sigrid and then uttered a goodbye over her shoulder to Matthew as she hurried back to Jed.

Jed was leaning against a tree. "What happened?"

"Seems he's innocent today. He's meeting someone."

Jed laughed.

Krystal frowned as she looked over and saw Matthew and Sigrid talking. "It's not funny!"

"It kind of is."

Krystal smiled, seeing the funny side. "Let's get out of here."

"I'm all for it."

As they drove away in the buggy, Krystal noticed Jed was looking over at her every so often. "What is it?" she asked with a hint of playfulness.

"I'm just admiring how gorgeous you are," he replied warmly.

Receiving such compliments was unfamiliar. Not knowing what to say, Krystal remained silent.

"Did I hear you tell Matthew you are in love with me?" he asked.

Krystal froze. "You heard that?"

"I did." He chuckled.

"I had to stop him from following us. Well, seems I didn't need to say that at all seeing that he was there for Sigrid."

Krystal was embarrassed that Jed heard her declaration of love even if it was how she felt. She couldn't believe she had said it out loud, and to Matthew of all people. "I'm sorry you had to hear that." She looked down at her lap.

"Don't be sorry. Maybe one day you'll say it to me."

She looked over at him and their eyes met. "Maybe."

MATTHEW COULD NOT HELP but watch Krystal and Jed together. Could Krystal's words be right? Was Sigrid interested in Andrew?

"Matthew."

He turned around to see Sigrid. "How are you?"

"I am doing well. But before you say anything, I want to get something off my chest."

Matthew realized this would be his last chance to make amends with Sigrid. She would drift away and marry Andrew if he didn't express his feelings. He had to seize the moment before she told him about Andrew.

"No, please. I have something to say," Matthew said eagerly.

"Alright, but let me go first—"

He interrupted her. "I shouldn't have gotten mad at you for what happened. I know now that you were pushed into that stupid scheme to trap me. I forgive you now. God brought us together, regardless of context or how things ended up, and we fell in—"

"Matthew, please. Stop. It's over between us. I'm here to tell you that I'm no longer interested in a relationship with you. Goodbye." She turned and started walking away.

Matthew was amazed that she didn't even have the decency to tell him about Andrew. He ran to catch up with her. "Who is he? I know there's someone else."

She stopped to talk with him. "Not that it's any of your business, but I guess you'll find out sooner rather than later. Andrew Weeks."

Matthew tipped his hat back on his head. "I don't recall ever seeing you two talk before."

"We hadn't spoken until we bumped into each other at Adam's birthday dinner at Wilma's house."

Matthew was taken aback. He hadn't heard about a dinner. He also missed going to Wilma's house for meals. Obviously, he hadn't been to Wilma's in a while; ever since he started having problems with Krystal. "When was this birthday dinner?"

"Not too long ago, and just by coincidence, I was sitting next to Andrew."

A deep sadness overcame him. His aunt and Wilma had conspired against him, given that he wasn't invited to the birthday dinner. That had to have been deliberate. "I get it." He hung his head. Everyone was against him.

"I must be going now, Matthew. Don't be too sad."

"Why wouldn't I be? I've lost you."

She looked down at the ground and then looked back at him. "I'm not perfect. I'm rather imperfect. I never told you this, but I would've if we got to talking about marriage. You see, the thing is, I can't have children."

He stared at her for a moment, taking in her words. "What do you mean?"

Sigrid shrugged her shoulders. "I just can't have babies."

"How would you know that?"

"It's a medical thing. And it's for sure. It's something I have to live with and whoever marries me will remain childless."

"I had no idea." He shook his head, feeling sorry for her and whomever she married.

"No. Why would you have any idea? I don't go around telling people, but I thought it might make you feel better. Perhaps you had a lucky escape. Bye, Matthew."

"Yeah, bye." Matthew took off his hat and stayed where he was until Sigrid was out of sight. He did want a family of his own. He'd always imagined himself sitting at the head of a large table, after a hard day's work, with ten or twelve children seated around it. His wife would lovingly serve the meal while the older children helped.

Sigrid couldn't have been the right one for him. He knew that now. He had to have children. That's what life was all about—family.

He thought again about his aunt betraying him. Perhaps God had His hand in that too. He wouldn't want to be in Andrew Week's shoes.

As he walked back to his horse and buggy, Matthew couldn't help but feel lost.

CHAPTER 23

avor made her very first meal in their very own kitchen. It was a meal for two. Their house was finished enough for them to have moved in. The meal was chicken with salad and fruit salad with cream for dessert.

It didn't matter that the meal was nothing special. What mattered was they were finally alone.

As Simon and Favor finished the dessert, Simon looked at Favor. "How do you feel?"

She knew what he meant. He was just as happy as she was. "I've just made a meal without any input from your mother. I'm feeling satisfied."

Simon chuckled. "It is good without the tension."

Favor smiled back, feeling a sense of comfort she hadn't felt in a long time. She leaned in closer to Simon, resting her head on his shoulder. "I want to do things without feeling like I'm being judged or criticized all the time."

"I know. I'm just glad you had the strength to endure what they put you through. I know it wasn't easy at times." Simon placed a gentle kiss on the top of her head.

"Thank you for seeing that. It means a lot."

Simon looked around the room. "We've made this place our own, and it's our sanctuary."

"We'll be so happy here. I know it."

Simon nodded in agreement, but there was something else on his mind. "There's something I've been wanting to discuss with you," he said, his voice serious.

Favor raised an eyebrow and sat up straight. "What is it?"

He inhaled deeply before continuing. "I know we've been trying for a baby for a while now, and it hasn't happened. And I've been thinking, and maybe we should try IVF. Have you heard of it?"

Favor's heart skipped a beat at the mention of their lack of a child after being married for years. "I have heard of it, and I've also heard it's expensive."

Simon breathed out heavily. "Really?"

Favor nodded. "And I'm pretty sure before that happens, they'll need to run some tests on both of us to see what they can find. There could be something simple stopping us from getting pregnant."

"Let's do those tests and then go from there."

Favor nodded. "Okay. We've jumped one huge hurdle to get here, so this next hurdle will be nothing in comparison."

Simon grinned, feeling a renewed sense of hope.

"Great, I'll book an appointment with the doctor tomorrow."

"Should you check with the bishop first? I don't know if I've heard anyone in the community going down this route."

"We're not going down it yet. We're investigating our options."

Favor's smile grew wider as she leaned in to kiss him. "Thank you," she said, grateful again for Simon's support.

As they cuddled on the couch, watching the fire after their meal, Favor couldn't help but feel excited and nervous about the prospect of starting a family after so long. She had always dreamed of being a mother, but the thought of going for tests was daunting.

Simon sensed her apprehension and squeezed her hand. "We'll do this together," he reassured her. "And no matter what happens, we'll always have each other."

"What if something is wrong and we can't have children?"

"We'll deal with it."

"How?"

"We'll get a couple of dogs. No big deal." He chuckled, and Favor was comforted by his words.

As they settled in for the night, she couldn't help but think this next chapter in their lives would be their greatest adventure yet.

~

THE FOLLOWING DAY, Favor opened her eyes to see Simon placing a tray of breakfast and a large mug of coffee on the bed beside her. "Good morning," she said as she pushed herself up.

"Morning." He sat beside her.

"What's the time?"

"It's late, but I thought you needed the sleep."

She rubbed her eyes. "No animals to feed, no fences to mend. What will you do today?"

He shrugged his shoulders. "I need to find some work to tide us over until we figure out what to do with our land."

Favor put the coffee up to her lips and took a sip. She didn't care what they had to do as long as they were away from Simon's controlling parents. She looked down at the bacon and eggs. "Thanks for this. It looks amazing."

"You're amazing, and from now on, I'll make you breakfast in bed every morning."

Favor was delighted to hear it. "You can't say that. You might have to wake early and go to work or something."

"I'll do it before I go as long as it won't be too early for you."

Favor smiled warmly. "That sounds perfect. I'm not sure I want to make an appointment with the doctor today. I don't want to do anything. I want one day to fully enjoy each other and our house. Can we do that?"

He leaned over and kissed her forehead. "Anything you want. One day won't make a difference."

She looked down at her breakfast. "Have you had any yet?"

"I've already eaten."

"Then I'll do the washing up."

He laughed. "Only if I help. Let's do everything together today for our first day of togetherness."

"I love that idea." Favor finished her breakfast, and they got up to clean the dishes together.

A knock sounded on the front door as Favor put the last dish away.

Simon looked up from folding the dish towel. "Who could that be?"

"One of our neighbors, most likely. Let's answer the door together." Favor headed to the door with a spring in her step while Simon followed. She opened the door, and she couldn't believe what she saw.

It was them!

Simon moved closer and opened the door fully. "What are you doing here?"

CHAPTER 24

"*S*urprise," Harriet and Melvin chorused as they made their way into Favor and Simon's house.

Surprise? Favor could think of a few other words, and surprise was not among them.

"Oh, what a lovely couch. Look, Melvin," Harriet made herself comfortable on their new couch.

Melvin sat beside her and bounced up and down a couple of times. "Very nice. Good springs."

Simon opened his mouth and then looked at Favor. She gave him her best pleading look. He had to do something about this. "Ma, Pa, didn't we say we'd let you know when we were settled, and then you could visit us?"

A smile brightened Harriet's face. "We know that, and you said we could eventually move here when we sell our house. Right?"

Simon gave a nod. "That's correct."

"Ah yes, and we have some good news about that, don't we, Harriet?" Melvin beamed at his wife.

Favor held her head and remained silent. They couldn't have possibly sold the house so fast. She'd been told it could take years to sell.

Harriet nodded. "So, we didn't sell. We leased it. It all happened so fast that Melvin and I knew it was nothing more than a miracle."

For whom? Favor wanted to ask because it was undoubtedly no miracle for her, Simon, or their marriage.

This was a disaster. "Where will you stay?" Favor asked, trying to sound cheerful. "We only have two bedrooms here. The second one is full of building materials still."

"Favor and I have every intention of building onto this house, but until then, it's so small."

"Don't worry. We won't be staying here, will we, Melvin?"

"No." Melvin shook his head. "We know you want to be alone. We will find a place to stay for a while, and then we might lease something. Unless... are there any other blocks for sale around here like yours? I hear they're going cheap."

Favor felt a knot form in her stomach at the thought of her in-laws staying nearby. She had hoped their move would provide them with some much-needed distance from them. She looked at Simon, and he looked just as helpless as she felt.

They couldn't turn them away.

"I'm not sure if there's land for sale. We'll have to check with the locals about somewhere for you to lease." Simon cleared his throat and added, "We'll help you find a place, but it might take a while. In the meantime, we can make some room for you here.

Harriet looked around. "It's small, but small is cozy."

"Thank you, Simon and Favor," Melvin said, his eyes brightening. "We really appreciate it."

"It didn't take us long to miss you. We missed you the moment you drove away, didn't we, Melvin?"

"We did. For sure."

Favor wondered how long it would've taken her to miss her in-laws. Maybe a year, perhaps two or three?

"You don't mind us staying here, do you, Favor?" Harriet asked.

Even though Favor was yet to have one day alone with Simon in their new place, she could never allow anyone to feel unwelcome in her home. "It'll be fun. We lived with you for so long. We can host you until you find a suitable place." *Hopefully, that will be super quick,* Favor thought.

Melvin clapped his hands. "Well, now that's settled, why don't we all go into town for some lunch? My treat."

Simon and Favor exchanged a look before nodding their agreement. It would give them some time to figure out what to do next.

Thank you for reading A Chance for Love.

www.SamanthaPriceAuthor.com

THE NEXT BOOK IN THE SERIES

The next book in the series is Book #37:
Her Amish Wish

The Baker/Bruner family look forward to a new beginning with newborn babies and blossoming relationships. Florence has added another baby to her family and couldn't be happier. Wilma, Ada, and their friends diligently prepare for Debbie's special day when an unwelcome visitor arrives.

Meanwhile, Matthew tries to figure out what he has done wrong in his interactions with women. He makes a bold move to win back a lost love. Will it pay off?

ABOUT SAMANTHA PRICE

Samantha Price is a USA Today bestselling and Kindle All Stars author of Amish romance books and cozy mysteries. She was raised Brethren and has a deep affinity for the Amish way of life, which she has explored extensively with over a decade of research.

She is mother to two pampered rescue cats, and a very spoiled staffy with separation issues.

www.SamanthaPriceAuthor.com

THE AMISH BONNET SISTERS

Book 10 Amish Bliss

Book 11 Amish Apple Harvest

Book 12 Amish Mayhem

Book 13 The Cost of Lies

Book 14 Amish Winter of Hope

Book 15 A Baby for Joy

Book 16 The Amish Meddler

Book 17 The Unsuitable Amish Bride

Book 18 Her Amish Farm

Book 19 The Unsuitable Amish Wedding

Book 20 Her Amish Secret

Book 21 Amish Harvest Mayhem

Book 22 Amish Family Quilt

Book 23 Hope's Amish Wedding

Book 24 A Heart of Hope

ALL SAMANTHA PRICE'S SERIES

Amish Maids Trilogy

Amish Love Blooms

Amish Misfits

The Amish Bonnet Sisters

Amish Women of Pleasant Valley

Ettie Smith Amish Mysteries

Amish Secret Widows' Society

Expectant Amish Widows

Seven Amish Bachelors

Amish Foster Girls

Amish Brides

Amish Romance Secrets

Amish Christmas Books

Amish Wedding Season

Made in the USA
Middletown, DE
21 February 2024

50100000R00116